My eyes stung all of a sudden. I started to panic. Maybe it had something to do with the electrical shock. Would I go blind? I wiped my forehead. I was drenched. And then I realized my heart was pounding a million miles an hour.

I took a few deep breaths and tried to relax. "Incredible," I whispered. I could see what my computer was doing at home *and* operate it all the way from school—just by *thinking* the commands. I kept thinking this was a dream and that I would wake up and be back to normal.

I almost wished I would.

But not quite....

CyberShock

Totally Wired

The
Computer
in Jed's
Head

David Lambert

digital cover illustration by Michael Petty

With love to Anna and Beth,
the brightest lights in
Lincoln, Nebraska

Published by Worthington Press
801 94th Avenue North, St. Petersburg, Florida 33702

Copyright © 1996 by Worthington Press,
a division of PAGES, Inc.

Printed in the United States of America

2 4 6 8 10 9 7 5 3 1

ISBN 0-87406-741-3

Chapter. 1

Okay, I know this is going to sound pretty weird. You probably won't believe it. But it's true, I swear.

The whole thing started with my dad yelling at me and waving my report card around. I was sitting at my desk, starting to take my computer apart to put in a couple of one-megabyte SIMMs. In case you don't know much about computers, SIMMs are memory chips. I was adding more memory to my computer's brain so it could run some serious software. My parents had bought me the computer, but I'd saved up my allowance and bought the SIMMs myself.

My dad was sitting on my bed. "You can't just play around all your life, Jed," he was saying.

All my life? I thought. *I'm in sixth grade, for Pete's sake. Gimme a break.* I got all the screws out and carefully lifted the back off the computer.

"There's a time for play," my dad said, "and there's a time for work, and these grades…" He tapped my report card. "These grades don't show much willingness to work. I know you're smart enough to get A's, Jed. But you'll be in junior high next year, and you still act as if math is just a joke."

Math is what we have computers for, Dad. Join the modern age. I could see the motherboard— the main circuit board where the memory chips are—behind a few cables and things. I carefully unplugged the end of one wide cable and moved it out of the way.

"Well, math is no joke. Your grades last year

were great, Jed."

Yeah, because last year I had Mr. Sloan.

"But this year you're spending all of your time on your computer—and not on your homework. There's nothing wrong with learning about computers. But school comes first. I want A's and B's by the end of the marking period, Jed, or you'll lose computer privileges."

Now he had my attention. "What?" I said.

"You heard me." He put the report card down on the bed and looked at me with his I-really-mean-this look. "If I don't see some real improvement in your grades on your next progress report, I'll move that computer out of your room, and you'll be able to use it only for homework."

"Dad—"

"That's the way it's going to be, Jed. The grades come up—and fast—or the computer goes."

"All because of a couple of lousy math grades?"

"It isn't just math, Jed. None of your grades

are what they should be, in any subject." He looked at my report card again and rolled his eyes. "Except gym."

This was serious. Sure, I could get the grades if I wanted to. But that would mean time away from my computer, and I couldn't handle that.

You see, computers are my *life!* Computers and sports, anyway. If Dad took my computer away, I'd go crazy or something. I mean, I've got animation programs—I can take a picture or a photo and make it move like a cartoon. I've got a modem that hooks up my computer to the phone lines. That means I can call the numbers of other computers or online services. We subscribe to a service called ByteLine that has sports scores, an encyclopedia, and all kinds of games and stuff. Plus on ByteLine you can go into these things called "discussion rooms" and "talk" by typing messages back and forth to people you don't even know. It's great! I'm not sure why kids even have to go to school anymore, except to keep us out of our parents' hair. I mean, we don't *need* school anymore. We have computers!

I turned back toward my desk. There sat those new memory chips, waiting to be installed. I pushed the wide cable out of the way again and slowly reached in to pull out the motherboard.

"I'll tell you this," Dad went on, "and I know what I'm talking about. Whatever career you choose—Jed!" he yelled, and just as he yelled, there was this incredibly bright flash, like it was right inside my brain, and smoke and this odd tinny smell and this very strange sound, like *bzzzzzzzZAP!* And then everything got real foggy and black. I felt like I was falling.

Through the fog I could hear my dad's voice: "Jed! Jed, are you okay? *Honey, get in here!* Jed?"

It seemed like a long time before I could open my eyes. I was lying on my back. Both my parents were bending over me. They had these real worried looks on their faces. "Honey, are you okay?" my mom asked.

"What happened?" I said. My voice sounded weird, like it wasn't coming out of my body.

"You almost fried yourself," my dad said.

"How? I unplugged the computer before—"

"Yes, but even when it's unplugged, the anode at the base of the cathode-ray tube retains a charge of several thousand volts. It's supposed to be covered by a plastic cap so nobody touches it accidentally, but the plastic cap was loose. I noticed it just before you touched it. Follow my finger with your eyes."

Then my dad, who's a doctor, went through all the stuff doctors do to make sure you're all right. When he was finished he said, "You're pretty lucky, sport. That's a lot of juice. Luckily, it's just a one-time jolt. Once it discharges into your body, it's over."

"What about my computer?" I asked.

My mom shook her head. "Is that all you can think of?" she said, sitting down on the bed.

My dad helped me stand up. The two of us sat at my desk while my dad carefully put everything back together, plugged the computer in, and then switched it on.

What a relief! I could see the start-up screen I always use:

Yo, Jed! You turn me on!

Then my dad said something that really blew me away. "I was afraid of that," he said. "It hums, but there's nothing on the screen. CRT must have burned out. Sorry, guy. Maybe we can get it replaced this week."

What's he talking about? I thought. *It works fine. At least, the start-up screen came up.* I looked at my dad, and this is where everything gets really weird. Written across Dad's face, right across his glasses and everything, was my start-up screen message:

Yo, Jed! You turn me on!

I shoved my chair away from the desk, slapped my hands over my eyes, and yelled, "Aaaah!"

My dad reached out and grabbed my shoulders so hard he almost lifted me right out of my chair. "What's wrong?" he and my mom said at the same time.

I split my fingers just a bit and looked away from my dad toward the window shade.

Yo, Jed! You turn me on!

I stared at my Nebraska Cornhuskers football poster.

Yo, Jed! You turn me on!

It was in my head! Everywhere I looked, I could see what was supposed to be on my computer screen. The screen was in my head!

Whoa! This was very strange. "Mom!" I yelled.

"What, honey? What's wrong? Are you in pain?"

"No. Just look at Dad's face and tell me—"

"Because you're very pale. Are you sure you're okay?"

"I'm sure! I'm pale because I just got electrocuted. Could you just look at Dad's face and tell me what you see?"

She looked. Dad looked back at her. "I see your dad." They both looked at me, very strangely.

"Now look at my computer screen and tell me what you see."

Like trained monkeys, they both looked at the computer screen. "Nothing," my mom said.

"A blank screen. Just like your dad said."

"Okay. Just wanted to make sure."

My mom put her hand on my forehead. "You sure you're feeling all right?"

It was in my head. My computer screen was in my head—and nobody else could see it!

"Why don't I make you some eggnog?" she asked. Eggnog. That's her cure for everything, year-round. Got a broken leg, just drink a quart of Mom's fresh homemade eggnog and you'll be back in the game by halftime.

"No thanks, Mom," I said. "Really. I'm okay." All I wanted was to be alone for a few minutes to think this through. "Maybe I'll just lie down for a while."

Mom wasn't ready to give up yet. "Frank," she said, "maybe we should take him to the emergency room."

"I don't think so," Dad said calmly. One thing about having a doctor for a dad—you don't question his judgment. If he said I was okay, I was okay. Period. "I just checked everything they'd check there," he said, "and he checks out fine. It's normal to be tired under these circumstances." He motioned Mom toward the door and stood up. "Just rest for a while, sport. We'll call you for dinner."

Chapter. 2

When their footsteps died off down the stairs, I crept quietly over to my computer. Dad had forgotten to turn it off since he couldn't see anything on the screen.

I turned up the brightness control. Yep—the image in front of my eyes got brighter. I looked up at the ceiling and turned the dial up and down a couple of times. The image brightened and dimmed. "Incredible," I whispered. I was wired, all right. I could see the real world and the computer screen at the same time. *Like a window,* I thought. *It's like looking at the real world through a window, and on that window is my computer screen. Very strange.*

I shut my eyes. The screen image was still there—just reversed, like a negative, light against dark.

I pulled a graphics disk out of my disk file and pushed it into the disk drive. I opened the program and started using it to draw some random curves. Amazing! I could see it all!

My eyes stung all of a sudden. At first I started to panic. Maybe it had something to do with the electrical shock. Would I go blind? I was about to holler for my dad when I realized it was just sweat dripping into my eyes. I wiped my forehead. I was drenched. Why? I hadn't been doing anything. And then I realized my heart was pounding a million miles an hour. I had to calm down. I leaned back and watched the curves scroll lazily across the ceiling.

Relax, I told myself. *You're just weirded out. You'll get used to it. It'll be great. But first you've got to stop sweating before you drown. Breathe deep.*

In. Out.

While I was doing that, I got tired of the curves. *I bet that animation program would look really good this way,* I thought. *Especially that file I made out of that picture of the bird, where its wings flap—*

Suddenly the curves disappeared. Now that crazy bird appeared out of nowhere and flapped across my ceiling.

I jumped backwards, pushed my chair clear over, and crashed to the floor.

Then I heard footsteps running up the stairs.

I leaped back into the chair and scattered a couple of books across the carpet just a second before my mom threw open the door. "What happened?" she gasped.

"Oh—you heard that?" I said innocently.

"Heard it? It sounded as if you were about to come through the ceiling!" That's one of my mom's favorite expressions, even though I've never actually heard of anyone falling through the ceiling. "Did you fall out of your chair?"

"Uh…" I hate it when she asks direct

questions like that because I don't like to lie to her. I'd rather just tell the truth in a way that isn't exactly the whole truth. That way, I'm not really lying. "I dropped these books." That was true, right?

She looked at me suspiciously. "Have you been sweating? Your hair's wet. How do you feel?"

I wiped my damp hair. "Yeah, it is a little wet. All the excitement, I guess. I feel okay."

She squinted at me for a few seconds and then slowly pulled the door closed, saying "Dinner in fifteen minutes" just before it clicked.

I collapsed back into my chair and listened to my heart pound. I shook my head hard. I had activated the animation program without touching the computer! All I'd done was think it. I had imagined, without even realizing it, the commands it would take to get to the flying bird file. And the computer had responded exactly as if I had typed in each of the commands!

I decided to try it again. I put my hands in my pockets and concentrated.

Close graphics program.

It closed!

Eject disk.

The disk ejected!

"Whoa," I whispered.

Now, the obvious question: Do I tell my parents? The equally obvious answer: Not yet. They'd think I was crazy.

Besides, what had my dad been waving in my face when this whole thing happened? And what was he threatening to take away if I didn't make those grades look a lot better by the next progress report? There was no reason to fail another test or give another wrong answer in school—ever. *If* I could keep the computer in my head a secret, of course. That wasn't exactly honest, I admit, but I had to consider what was at stake. I *had* to keep my computer. And now I had found a way to do just that.

The next day, Monday, we were having a math test on fractions and decimals. Good thing my computer has a special high-speed math co-processor.

Dad will be plenty proud of the grade I'll get on <u>this</u> math test, I thought. *As long as he doesn't know how I got it.*

Chapter. 3

It was scary, man. I mean, it was *scary*.

I sat there with the math test on my desk, afraid to answer the first question. I kept expecting Mrs. Wright to jump up and say, "Aha! Jed, you obviously have a computer in your brain. I'm going to call the police."

So I looked at the first question for about five minutes.

1. Convert the following to decimals. Round your answer to four decimal places.

A. 23/82.

It was now or never. I looked up at Mrs. Wright. She smiled. I waited until she looked away—don't ask me why—and then I mentally called up the calculator function of my math program, typed in the numbers, and ta-da! There was the answer. I wrote it down:

.2805.

Incredible! I wiped my forehead and realized I was sweating again. I could feel my heart thumping. I hoped this wouldn't happen every time I used my head-computer.

By the time I got halfway through the first list of fractions, I realized I was racing through them like I was trying to win a prize. I knew I couldn't turn my paper in early. That would be sure to make Mrs. Wright suspicious. So I closed my eyes and took a couple of deep breaths, waited a minute or two, and then finished the test slowly. As it turned out, I didn't get done that much ahead of everybody else, and I waited until a few others had turned in their papers before I took mine up.

Mrs. Wright smiled at me again as I put my

paper on her desk. No suspicious glare, no scowl, no frown—it was obvious she didn't suspect a thing. Not yet, anyway.

We were supposed to begin our reading assignment while we waited for the period to end. Mrs. Wright started grading the tests. When the bell rang, she looked up and said, "Oh, Jed, would you stay just a minute, please?"

This is it. I'm dead, I thought. I shuffled up to her desk. I felt like I should stick out my wrists for her to slap the cuffs on. While everybody else filed out of the room, she just kept her head down, looking at my paper, and let me stand there. I stared at the gray bun on the back of her head, each hair tucked in perfectly. She's kind of funny, Mrs. Wright. She's got to be the oldest teacher at Livermore, but she's tall and she looks strong enough to pick you up with one hand.

A couple of kids peered back inside through the big windows to see if I was getting into trouble, but Mrs. Wright glared at them until they ran out onto the soccer field. Then she turned to me—and smiled!

"Congratulations, Jed," she said, and held up my paper for me to see. There was a big red "100%" at the top.

I didn't know what to say, so I just stared. She laughed. "Surprised?" she said. "Well, I'm not. I knew you could do it, Jed. I'll admit your math grades haven't been very good so far this year. In fact…" She looked in her grade book. "You haven't had above a seventy-five until today." She cocked an eyebrow at me. "And we both know why that is."

"Yes, ma'am."

"You haven't been trying."

"Yes, ma'am."

"But I know from talking to Mr. Sloan what kind of work you are capable of, and I've just been waiting for you to start working up to your ability. I'm glad to see that day has finally come."

She just sat there, smiling, like she was waiting for me to say something. Finally I said, "Mrs. Wright, I'm supposed to be the soccer captain in gym class. Can I go?"

She laughed. "Yes, heaven forbid I should

keep you from soccer. Thank you, Jed."

I grabbed my coat and ran out the door. I should have felt relieved and happy about acing the test. And I guess I did. But in another way I felt bad. Mrs. Wright was being so nice about it, and she was feeling so happy for me, when really what I was doing was—well, I felt weird.

I chose my team and we took the field. It was a pretty warm day for February. I ended up taking off my coat. No clouds, wide blue sky, a little bit of wind. We'd had several days of weather like this. All the snow had melted and most of the mud had dried up. Usually I played goalie, but I played midfielder today because I had a hunch I wouldn't really have my mind on the game. I was right. I played lousy.

"Come on, Vanderlaan!" Todd Jackson yelled at me after I let this little shrimpy guy steal the ball from me. "Wake up!"

Fat chance. I had so many things going through my head I couldn't concentrate on the game. Like what Mrs. Wright had said about Mr. Sloan. So the teachers sat around and talked about us. That was weird.

Mr. Sloan had been my fifth-grade teacher last year. He was the kind of teacher everybody at the whole school knew. Even the second graders would say, "I want Mr. Sloan when I'm in fifth grade." He did lots of little things, like he'd have a new riddle every day. They weren't always good ones, but that didn't matter. The bad ones were more fun, really. We'd all groan when he told one.

Today's test had been my first A since leaving Mr. Sloan's class. I got lots of A's last year, but that was different. I didn't mind doing homework or studying for Mr. Sloan. He actually made the work seem interesting—even fun. And since everybody else in the class felt the same way, I didn't feel like I was being a geek or something to study for a test or get a report done on time.

So now I could get A's again.

And then when the teachers sat around and talked about me, Mrs. Wright could tell Mr. Sloan I was "working up to my ability" again.

Then he'd be happy for me.

For some reason, though, I didn't want Mr. Sloan to hear about all this.

I missed a pass and the ball bounced out of bounds. Eric Swanson whacked me with his baseball cap and sneered, "Nice going, *captain*."

Chapter. 4

"**H**ey, Vanderlaan!" Todd Jackson called as soon as we stepped into the hallway after school was over. He shouldered his way toward me through the crowd of kids. His buddies Eric Swanson and Tony Palmiero were right behind him. "How'd you do it?"

"Do what?" I said.

"You know what," Eric said. "Next time you get test answers ahead of time, cut me in."

So they'd seen my score when Mrs. Wright was handing the math tests back. "You guys serious?" I said. "You think I needed to cheat to ace that stupid test?"

They laughed. "Yeah," Todd said, "that's what we think. Hey!" he yelled at the mass of kids crowding around us. "Give us some room, would ya?" Todd is Mr. Popularity, and everybody wanted to hear what he was saying. Great. Just what I needed. I could hear some of the kids whispering, "Jed got an A on the math test!"

Alan Ward squeezed through right behind Todd and held up his wrist, tapping his watch. We had a fund-raising committee meeting to go to. Every sixth grader at Livermore is expected to be on some kind of committee or do some service project. Alan and I had chosen the fund-raising committee for one reason only—Mr. Sloan was the teacher adviser.

"Come on, Vanderlaan," Eric said. "You never get above a C. Now all of a sudden you get a hundred percent? Just tell us how you did it. We're not gonna tell."

Alan started waving his arms. We didn't have

much time for the meeting, because Myra Steinmetz's mom—Myra was the other member of the committee, and usually a royal pain—came to pick us up at three-thirty. "I gotta go," I said.

Todd and Eric shook their heads, smirking. But they moved aside, and Alan and I started fighting our way through the crowd to Mr. Sloan's room.

"So how *did* you get that A?" Alan asked. Alan's a little weird. He's kind of a brain, he wears really strange clothes, he's a disaster at sports, and he sings in the school chorus. But he's a good guy and we've been friends since first grade. After all, it's not like I was Mr. Social Success or anything myself.

"Alan, it's no big deal. You're just like Todd and those guys. You think I'm not smart enough to get—"

"We all *know* you're smart enough. You just don't *care* enough. Big difference. So what's the deal? Did you cheat?"

We were almost at Mr. Sloan's room by that

time. I could see Myra standing in the doorway. When she saw us coming, she looked at her watch. "Drop dead, Ward," I said, and we followed Myra into the room.

The three of us sat at a round table, nobody saying anything. Myra was upset because—well, because Myra was *always* upset. And Alan—I mean, what did he want? I felt weird enough about this whole deal without him giving me a hard time. But I had no choice, right? What was I supposed to do, let my dad take away my computer?

Mr. Sloan rushed in. "Sorry I'm late," he said, pulling out a chair and dropping into it. "Let's get to it. I know you guys have to leave soon."

By the time he sat down, I was feeling better about everything. Mr. Sloan just makes you feel that way. He's tall and built like an athlete, but he isn't what you'd call handsome or anything. He has kind of a pitted face and reddish blonde hair that sticks out where it isn't supposed to, and he wears wire-rimmed glasses that are sometimes kind of twisted and crooked from wrestling with his kids. He's a pretty ordinary dresser. But it isn't his looks that make us all like him so much, anyway.

It's hard to explain. He pays attention to you. He makes things fun. He makes you feel like you're important—like there isn't anyplace he'd rather be or anybody else he'd rather be with.

He tossed a couple of packets on the table. "I got these in the mail from the gift-wrap place. We did pretty well selling wrapping paper last year. Think we ought to do the same thing this year?"

"Before we decide that," Myra said, "can we go over what we've made so far this year?"

He looked surprised. "Can we what?"

"I just want to see how we're doing compared to last year," she said.

Myra is Miss Competition. She always wants to be better than everybody else at everything.

"Oh," Mr. Sloan said. "Yeah, sure. But let's not do that right now. We don't have all that much time."

"Don't you have that stuff on computer?" Alan said. "It should be easy to just—"

"Whoa, pardner," Mr. Sloan said. He seemed impatient, which was odd. "Yeah, it's all on computer, but the way it's entered, it would take a while to compare the two years." Then he grinned, as if trying to lighten things up. "That's all. No big deal. We'll do it another day."

Alan and I looked at each other, forgetting our fight for a minute. This was kind of weird. It didn't matter how the information was entered. Mr. Sloan could pull it out fifteen different ways if he wanted to. He's a real computer whiz. In fact, he's the one who got Alan and me into computers last year. So why didn't he just pull out the data on the two years to keep Myra happy? It didn't make sense.

There was a knock, and we all turned toward the doorway. There stood Mr. Halston, the principal. He's a short guy, with gray spiky hair. He looks like an ex-marine. "Just a reminder," he growled at Mr. Sloan. "Those grading reports are due to me tomorrow, first thing."

Mr. Sloan saluted. "Tomorrow first thing, *sir!*" We tried not to grin.

Mr. Halston opened his mouth to say something, but then another guy stepped up behind him. I'd seen the other guy around school a couple of times before, but I didn't know who he was. He had thick glasses and cool clothes that looked kind of out of place on his pudgy body.

Mr. Sloan nodded at him. "Hello, Mr. Garfield."

"How ya doin'?" the other man mumbled, not smiling. His voice sounded wheezy. Then he turned to Mr. Halston. "You want to go over those invoices now?" he said.

The two of them walked off down the hall.

"Who's he?" Myra asked.

"He's a computer technician," Mr. Sloan said, opening up the information packets on the table and spreading the brochures and gift-wrap samples all around. "He tunes up all the computers in the school district. Smart guy. He was probably like you when he was in school,

Jed. Smart enough to get straight A's, but he spent all of his time playing with computers."

"Jed got an A today," Alan said. I wanted to punch him. "One hundred percent."

Mr. Sloan gave me a thumbs-up sign. "All right, Jed! What on?"

"Math test," Myra said, sneering. "He probably cheated."

"Now, Myra," Mr. Sloan said. "Jed's smart enough to get A's without cheating if he wants to."

What I wanted was to get out of there, fast. *Maybe I should just forget the whole deal,* I thought. *Somebody's gonna catch me. I just know it.* What a spooky situation. The whole time I was taking that test I felt all shaky and nervous. Partly because I was scared I'd get caught and partly because—well, the whole thing was weird. I could see what my computer was doing at home *and* operate it all the way from school. I kept thinking this was a dream and that I would wake up and be back to normal.

I almost wished I would.

But not quite. I guess it was more tempting than it was scary. So I made an A on my history test and an A on the science quiz. And Todd and Eric and Tony and Alan and Myra—and probably everybody else in the class, too—watched my every move. But they couldn't see anything, of course, because there was nothing to see. And I kept rolling up A after A after A. Within a week everybody started thinking I was some kind of genius.

Half the time, while class was going on all around me, I was checking out the discussion rooms on ByteLine and listening in while people who really knew their stuff talked about computers. Sometimes I checked the sports scores. What a kick!

There was just one problem. It was kind of boring doing it all by myself. It would have been more of a kick if I had someone to share it with.

On Friday night after dinner the phone rang. I answered it. "Hello."

"Jed? This is Myra."

The truth is, I didn't hate Myra as much as I pretended to. I'd just gotten into this name-calling thing with her. It had started as soon as she moved here from Chicago a couple of years ago. And now I couldn't really stop it. She was too smart and too good with words. She'd slice me to ribbons if I didn't defend myself.

I took the phone up to my room. "So what's up with fund-raising?" I asked.

"This isn't about fund-raising, Jed. Maybe it's just a nice social call. Don't you ever get nice social calls?"

"Yeah, but not from you." I sprawled across my bed.

"You're right about that. So what I really want to know is, are you cheating?" I could just hear the smirk in her voice.

"Myra—"

"I'm serious, Jed. You *could* be getting A's without cheating, but you haven't done serious work since Mr. Sloan's class. So if you're not cheating, tell me now, and I'll stop trying to figure out how you're doing it."

"Okay. I'm not cheating."

She didn't say anything for a while. Then she said, "Sorry, Jed, but I don't believe you."

"Well, then, why'd you call?"

"I don't know. Just to warn you, I guess. If you *are* cheating, I'll figure it out, Jed. I swear I will. It's a mystery. And I like mysteries. I'll keep at it until I solve it. In fact, I think I've already got it figured out. I'm just not sure how to test my theory yet."

Great. Myra is smarter than all the other kids I know—and brighter than most grown-ups too. If she was determined to figure me out, it was only a matter of time.

Chapter. 5

It turns out I'm lousy at keeping secrets. On Sunday night I told Alan about my head-computer. I just had to. It wasn't much fun doing all this incredible stuff by myself.

"Unbelievable," Alan said. He was sitting on my bed, staring straight ahead with this glazed look in his eyes.

It had taken me a half-hour to convince Alan that what I told him was true. He had run me through drill after drill, trying to trip me up. The last one he tried was to make me sit with my back to him while he typed different letters on the computer keyboard and asked me to guess them. I didn't miss a one, of course, because as soon as he hit the key, the letter appeared before my eyes.

"Utterly impossible."

"Yeah. But it's true," I said, grinning. I was sitting cross-legged on the floor, rocking back and forth. I felt a little hyper, like I needed to jump or shout or something. "So now that you know, you have to help me think of how to use this."

"This is absolutely the weirdest thing."

"I know, isn't it? But what do we do with it? You're a computer ace—what do you think?" And Alan *is* an ace—more than me, even. I just want to know what I can *do* with computers. But Alan wants to know everything *about* them. How they work, why, who's doing what with them, all that stuff. He's like Mr. Sloan.

"I can't believe it," he said. "This is completely and undeniably cool." He looked like he was in a trance or something. "A computer in your head. How utterly wild. How science fiction. Totally extraterrestrial." He looked at me with wide eyes. "Jed!" he yelled suddenly.

"Yell quietly," I whispered, "or you'll have my mom up here."

"My gosh, Jed, this is power!" he yelled just as loudly as before. "I mean, a good computer operator has power to spare anyway if he knows how to use what he's got. But to be able to sit and tap into the power of a computer *without anybody knowing it!* Jed, think about it!"

"Think about it?" I said. "What do you think I've been doing ever since it happened? I just haven't come up with any brilliant ideas yet."

"Do your parents know?" Alan asked.

What was he, nuts? "You kidding? They'd have me at the hospital hooked up to all kinds of machines inside of two minutes."

"Yeah, I guess you're right," Alan said.

"So tell me, wise one," I said, "what can we do with this? And don't tell me I can get A's. I already figured that out."

He laughed. "Well, yeah, you could, of course, but—" He stopped smiling. He looked at me really weird and said, "So you *were* cheating!"

"That wasn't cheating!"

"Of course it was! How is it any different from writing the answers on your hand like Eric did on that science test?"

"Because I didn't have to rely on anything other than what I had in my own head."

"Not true! You had to rely on the computer sitting in your bedroom. It's the same as if you had a little speaker in your ear and somebody outside of class was telling you the answers."

"Okay, okay. Let's skip the debate here. I just want to know what we can do with this thing."

"No way."

"What?"

"Forget it. You think you can just walk off with as many A's as you want to because you've got some freak computer thing going on in your head?"

I slugged his arm. "Who you calling a freak?"

"Ouch! Stop it!" He glared at me, and I walked over to the window.

"Hey," I said, looking out. "We could tap into the school's computer records and change grades, and just screw stuff up. You know. For fun."

"I can't believe you've been cheating," Alan said, rubbing his arm where I'd slugged him. "I thought maybe you just finally decided to use your brain for a change."

I was starting to get majorly ticked off. I spun around. "Will you just stop it with the righteous act? Are you saying that you wouldn't cheat if you had a computer in your brain?"

He shook his head. "No. I wouldn't."

I glared at him. "I'll bet you would if your dad told you he'd take your computer away—for real—if your grades didn't come up."

He thought that over. "Is that what happened?"

I nodded.

He thought some more. Then he said, "It wouldn't make any difference."

"Oh, yeah, right," I scoffed.

"You might try studying, Jed, just like everybody else."

"Just shut up, Alan. You sound like a parent. Okay, I *could* study, but I *need* that time! I spend it on ByteLine or learning new programs—"

"Hey, Jed, this is Alan you're talking to, all right? I'm as into computers as you are. But I have to work hard for my A's. It takes a lot of time, but I get the grade because I *deserve* it. And now I'm supposed to laugh and think it's funny that you're getting the grades without doing the work? Even though you're so smart that last year you got *better* grades than I did? It's not fair."

"Whine, whine, whine."

He got up, glaring at me. "Yeah, well, gee, I don't want to spoil your evening." And he stalked out.

Within two minutes, my mom was at my door. "Alan looked upset when he left," she said.

"You know how his ears get red. Did you boys have an argument?"

"No big deal," I said.

But as I lay in bed that night, telling myself it wasn't any of his business anyway, I kept hearing Alan say, "So you *were* cheating. So you *were* cheating. So you *were* cheating."

Chapter. 6

Mrs. Wright gave us a free half-hour after lunch the next day to read a couple of chapters out of our science book. I didn't bother. The test was the next day, but I had already figured out that everything in our science book was also in the online encyclopedia on ByteLine. Since I could tap into that during the test, I wasn't worried.

So while everybody else sat and read—except for Myra, who was using the computer at the back of the room to work on her social studies project—I signed on with ByteLine and went to "Hacker's Forum," the discussion room Alan and I usually go to when we just want to talk to somebody. It's always computer talk, but that's okay.

In these discussion rooms, whatever anybody types on his keyboard appears on the screen for everybody who's in that room to read. Each new comment shows up at the bottom of the list, right after the one before. So it's like having a conversation in a crowd where everybody can hear you and everyone else. Each person's screen name (mine's Jedediah) appears right before his comment, so you always know who's talking. It looks like the script of a play or something. You just learn to ignore all the comments you're not interested in.

I was reading the comments of two guys discussing a new optical hard drive, occasionally asking them a question of my own, when a comment appeared from someone named "MoreSmart."

MoreSmart: Jedediah, why aren't

you in school?

Whoa. This was weird. I decided to play it safe. I responded:

Jedediah: Sick today.

The answer came back:

MoreSmart: Can I call your parents and verify that?

Call my parents? Who *was* this? While I was figuring out what to answer, MoreSmart sent another message:

MoreSmart: You're scratching your ear.

I jerked my hand away from my ear, then looked quickly around to see who could be watching me. Another message came:

MoreSmart: Turn around.

I froze—then slowly turned around and looked at the back of the room. Myra sat there, smirking and pointing at me like she was a seven-foot NBA center who just slam-dunked in my face, as her next message flashed before me.

MoreSmart: GOTCHA! GOTCHA! GOTCHA!

Suddenly the door popped open, and Mr. Halston marched in, with the computer guy, Mr. Garfield, right behind him. They looked around the room without saying anything, and then spotted Myra sitting at the computer. "Excuse me, Mrs. Wright, but you have a student in this room using one of our modem lines at an unauthorized time," Mr. Halston said sternly.

Mrs. Wright looked surprised. "Myra," she began.

"Sorry, Mrs. Wright," Myra said. "Just needed to call into ByteLine to check some data. I didn't think it would be a problem."

"Well, it *is* a problem," Mr. Garfield growled. "We schedule student use of those computer lines for mornings only, because I use those lines for maintenance and servicing the system in the afternoon. Now you just messed up one of my tests and I'll have to run it again. You students need to remember that you only use the modems during the morning—"

"Excuse me, Mr. Garfield," Mrs. Wright said

huffily. "Thank you for pointing out the problem. Please leave the instruction of my students to me."

"Well, then, you tell 'em—"

"Thanks, Harry, I'll handle it from here," Mr. Halston said. "Mrs. Wright, be sure to remind your students that, as the sign in the media center clearly states, the phone lines attached to the computers are to be used only during morning hours. Mr. Garfield sometimes uses them for system maintenance in the afternoons." He glanced sternly at us, and then back at Mrs. Wright. "Be sure they understand." He and Mr. Garfield turned and marched out.

"Well!" Mrs. Wright stared angrily at the door for a few seconds. Then she said, "We've just had a little reminder. I'm sure nothing more needs to be said."

"Sorry, Mrs. Wright," Myra said again. She was talking to Mrs. Wright, but she was looking at me, and she looked plenty smug.

"It's quite all right, Myra. I'm sure you meant no harm."

Mrs. Wright was wrong about that. Myra had meant plenty of harm, but it had nothing to do with Mr. Garfield and his stupid tests.

I looked over at Alan. *Boy, have I got something to tell you,* I thought. *I think my life just got a whole lot more complicated.*

Chapter. 7

So later that day, I had to tell Myra too. When she heard my explanation, she just looked at me for a few seconds. Then she said, "You expect me to believe that?"

We were at Antelope Park, Myra and Alan and I, sitting on a picnic table we'd pulled up against the activities center trying to stay out of the wind. I'd chosen the place because I didn't want to take the chance that any parents might overhear us. The weather definitely felt like February then. I was glad I was wearing a heavy coat. Myra was wearing a dorky-looking parka that was too big for her and had fur around the hood. The sky was spitting a little snow, and the ground was frozen again.

It was almost dinnertime. It had taken me at least a half-hour to explain everything, mainly because Myra stopped me every minute or so with some question. I sighed. "I don't really care if you believe it, Myra. If you want to think I'm just a brain, fine. What *I'd* like to know is how you figured it out."

"It wasn't that hard," she said. "It was the classroom answers that gave you away. Anybody can get A's on tests if they study. But your answers in the classroom—I mean, some of Mrs. Wright's questions would be practically impossible to answer off the top of your head, and you answered them all right. I sat there thinking I'd have to memorize the almanac and the dictionary and the atlas to be able to answer all those questions. Either that or be sitting at my computer. Well, I didn't think you'd memorized the encyclopedia. So, obviously, you were somehow getting access to a computer—your home PC, I figured—while you were sitting in class. If that was true, I was sure I'd catch you in Hacker's Forum eventually. And I did. There's only one problem. I don't believe your explanation."

Stupid me. I should have given a couple wrong answers in class, just to keep things looking normal. "Yeah, well, great, Myra. If my story *isn't* true, what's *your* explanation? You watched me in class, so you know I wasn't using a laptop or anything."

She nodded, looking puzzled. "I know."

We sat silently for a few seconds, and then a gust of wind hit us and we all turned away from it. I'd had enough of this. "So, now that I've told you my little secret, why don't you just forget everything you heard and—"

"No way," she said. "I have no intention of forgetting about it. In fact, I have two questions for you right now. Question number one: Are you going to stop cheating?"

Oh, boy, I thought. *Here we go with the*

cheating thing again. "Don't you guys ever give up?" I said. "In the first place, it's none of your business, and—"

I didn't even get to finish that sentence. There was too much snorting and muttering from the two of them.

"That's about the stupidest thing I've ever heard," Myra said. "When somebody cheats in class, it affects everybody. We *compete* for grades, Jed, or hadn't you noticed? You're stealing somebody's A. I wouldn't mind you getting better grades than me if you worked for them, but I'm not going to let you get away with beating me by cheating."

"You what? You're not going to *let* me get away with it? Just how do you plan to stop me?"

"I'll stop you, all right. Never mind how. Just get used to the idea that you've cheated your last cheat."

"She's right, Jed," Alan said. "Give it up. It stinks. It really does."

"Listen…" I had to be careful how I explained this. I couldn't expect much sympathy from Myra. "My dad's gonna take away my computer if my grades don't come up. This way I can—"

I was right. No sympathy. "Gee, Jed, did you ever think of studying?" Myra asked sarcastically.

"Look, Myra. It's my head, it's my computer, and I'll use it any way—"

"Question number two," Myra interrupted. "What do you plan on doing with this ability now that you have it? Besides cheating in school, that is."

I was still sitting there with my mouth open, and I forgot to shut it. She had sure asked the right question.

"You haven't even figured out a plan yet?" Myra said.

"I never said that. Of course I have a plan," I said. "I mean, not a final one or anything, but first I'm going to get some decent grades and save my computer, and then—"

"You haven't even figured out a *plan* yet?" she repeated. "That's incredible. However you're doing this, you've got more power in your head than anybody in school—anybody in the world, probably—and the only thing you've figured out to do with it is to cheat on some tests that you could get A's on anyway if you'd just study. That's unbelievable, Jed. It really is. And that's why you're not going to cheat anymore."

"What?" I said. "What does that have to do with cheating?"

"Everything. Alan knows more about computers than you do, and I can think of at least a dozen good ways to use the computer in your head. You need us."

"I don't need anybody," I grumbled.

"You *need* us," she repeated, "and you know it. And we won't help you if you keep on cheating. Right, Alan?"

Alan looked at her for a few seconds, obviously not too happy about having to side with a girl against his best friend, but finally he nodded and said, "Right."

I glared at him. "Some friend."

He glared back. "Friends don't cheat each other."

When I didn't say anything for a while, Myra said, "Of course, I do have other options available to me."

Yeah, like telling Mrs. Wright or Mr. Halston, I thought.

Then Myra stood up and brushed off the seat of her jeans. "Well, it's been fun, guys, but I've got things to do. Alan, can I talk to you for a few minutes?"

The two of them walked off, talking quietly. I let them get as far as the sidewalk before I called out, "Hey, come back here a minute."

When they were sitting again, I said to Myra, "So, tell me about these ideas of yours for what I can do with this thing."

"What *we* can do," she corrected me.

Chapter. 8

"You kids meet me right here at eight-thirty," my mom called, disappearing into the crowd at the mall.

I watched her go, then grinned at Alan and Myra. "Let's get a soda," I said. This was Wednesday, one of the few nights my mom didn't have a class or a huge stack of homework. She's back in college, believe it or not, trying to get a degree. I have friends whose brothers or sisters are in college, but a mom?

We bought our drinks and found an empty

bench. I brushed some popcorn off the seat and flopped down. "You got it?" I said, poking my straw through the lid.

Myra smiled and pulled a little piece of paper out of her jeans pocket. "There are rewards for volunteering for office duty. You guys should try it sometime."

"Not likely. But," I said as I grabbed the paper, "we're glad you did." I looked at the scrap of paper. A phone number: 555-6854. The number of the school's computer system.

Mentally, I opened my communications program and started to dial the number. Myra interrupted. "Jed?" she said.

"What?"

"Are you doing it right now?"

"I'm dialing."

"Describe it to me. I mean, tell me what you're doing, what it looks like, what it feels like."

Describe it? Like a play-by-play? "Well, first I opened my communications program—"

"But how? I mean, how do you do it? Do

you just see the screen? Or what?"

There was mall music—schmaltzy orchestra versions of Beach Boys songs. "I can see the screen in front of my eyes," I said. "Like I'm looking at you through a window, and projected on that window is the screen of my computer."

"*All* the time you see the screen? Doesn't that get annoying?"

"I can mentally adjust the brightness control all the way down to zero if I don't want to see it."

"So how do you work it? How do you open the program?"

"I can move the cursor just by thinking it— up, down, however I want it to go. Instead of using the keyboard to give the commands, I just think them. So now I'm in the communications program, now I dial in the number…"

"But what does it *feel* like?" She tucked her long skinny legs up under her on the bench.

This was a different Myra. Usually she was so sarcastic, so mean, so—well, so much like me, I guess. But now she was talking to me like I was her friend. At that moment I realized, *She keeps everybody far away from her by acting like a witch. But she doesn't <u>have</u> to be like that. She can turn it on and off. And right now—just look at her face. It's like she's, I don't know, opening up to me or something. If I said something mean, I could really hurt her feelings. If I wanted to.*

"What does it feel like?" I said. "It's—it's like nothing I've ever felt before. It's really weird. It's scary. The first few times I did it, it made me sweat and shake." Myra's eyes were shining. She was studying my face, hanging on my every word—me, the kid nobody ever looked up to for anything. Myra Steinmetz was sitting there studying me like I was the only person in the world. I wanted to keep talking just to keep her like this.

So I did. "You know, I keep thinking other people can tell. Like that first test I used the computer on, that math test? I kept thinking Mrs. Wright would catch me."

I took a sip of my soda and tried to think of something else to say.

"Oh, wow," Alan said, sniffing the air like a dog.

"What?"

"Popcorn. You guys want some?"

I looked across the mall at the popcorn stand. "The line's a mile long, Alan. It'll take forever."

"No, it won't. I'll get cuts from somebody." And off he went, turning around when he was halfway there to shout back, "Don't do anything until I get back!"

"So what's happening now?" Myra asked, bright-eyed.

"I'm in," I said. "Start-up screen. Uh-oh."

"What?"

"It says, 'User ID.'"

"That just means initials. Use Halston's. RJH."

Mentally I typed in "RJH" and hit the enter key. "Now it wants a password." I looked up at her. "Do we need to guess?"

"Well…" Myra looked around. There was a bunch of high school kids standing a few feet away, just hanging out and laughing. It was obvious they weren't paying any attention to us. "His password is 'tiger.'"

Tiger? "Why 'tiger'?" I said.

She shrugged. "Who knows? Maybe that's the name of his cat. Just type it in and then forget where you heard it."

A couple of girls dressed all in black joined the group of teenagers beside us, and the noise level went up a whole bunch—shrieking and screaming and stuff. I talked louder. "Okay. Now I've got the main menu."

"What do you see?"

"'Utilities,' 'Administrative Functions,' all that. What should I get into?"

"There should be a database. NetWorld, I think. Open that."

"Okay. Got it. So, you want to get into the grading records, or what? Change a few grades around, just for fun?"

Myra shook her head, smirking. "Mr. Halston isn't stupid. He knows kids have modems. From working in the office, I know the grading records have a double password that only Mr. Halston and Mrs. Ortega know."

"We can figure it out," I said.

"You could waste a lot of time trying is more like it," she said, that sarcastic edge coming back into her voice. "But I've got a better idea. Let's tap into the fund-raising results and see how we're doing compared to last year."

I knew it. "My gosh, Myra, give it a rest. What's the big deal? Even if we're behind, we've got the rest of the semester—"

"I just want to know, okay?" she said. "If you don't, fine. I'll call in from my home computer and find out myself. I just thought this would be one way to test what we can do with—"

"All right, all right," I grumbled. "I need a password to get into the financial records."

"'Money.'"

"Figures. Hey, wow. Look at this—oh." We both laughed. I forgot she couldn't look. "We could get into all the salaries, all that sort of thing. Find out who's making what. We could—"

"Forget it, Jed. Fund-raising."

"Okay. Fund-raising. Geez. Let me look.... All right. Got it. Current year, first activity, saving Townline grocery receipts for the Thanksgiving dinner for the homeless. Total of a hundred twenty-seven dollars and forty-two cents. Second activity—"

Myra shook her head. "No, wait. That must have been just the fourth graders. Find the total."

"That is the total. It's all broken down by grades, and it shows total receipts, minus expenses, and that's what's left. There's a little note here that says a check for that amount went to the Lincoln Homeless Center on November twenty-first."

"No," Myra said, annoyed. "That's all messed up. The check must have been for five times that. What did the fifth grade make?"

"Forty-six bucks and fifty cents."

She shook her head. "That's crazy. I added up those slips myself and wrote the total down before I handed the stuff over to Mr. Halston. The fifth grade made over a hundred and eighty dollars. And the sixth grade made over two hundred. Tell me exactly what you see in the—"

"Myra, I know how to read the chart. And guess again. Sixth grade made fifty-two."

"That's not right, Jed," she said quietly. "Think. Don't you remember Mr. Sloan made some joke about taking the five hundred dollars and buying a ticket to Hawaii?"

I thought for a minute. "Vaguely," I said. "Yeah, I think I do remember that."

"There should have been over five hundred dollars for the homeless center," she said. "Read it to me again. Line by line."

I did. She put her feet back down on the ground and sat quietly for a minute or two, looking at her shoes. When she looked up, she was mad. "Jed, somebody stole four hundred dollars from the homeless account."

"Okay, look," I said. "Maybe it's just a mistake. I mean, maybe somebody just wrote down the wrong numbers. You remember how much we took in on the newspaper drive for the children's hospital?"

"Not exactly, but it was over seven hundred altogether."

"Wow. That much?"

"Yes. I had everybody at my church bring all their papers—over two hundred dollars' worth."

Figures. This girl was *competitive*. "Okay, the record says…" I closed my eyes to see it better. "One hundred ninety-six for the whole school."

"Jed!" She jumped up, walked halfway over to the Kasual Klothes store, her hands in fists, and then turned and stomped back. She threw herself back down on the bench and hissed, "Somebody is stealing this money! This money belongs to the homeless and to the children's hospital, and somebody is stealing it! If I ever find out who's doing this—"

Suddenly Alan came out of nowhere and plopped down between us. "Hey!" he said around a mouthful of popcorn. "Did I miss anything?"

Chapter. 9

Myra called the next night after dinner. "It's even worse than we thought, Jed," she said. "My mom remembered how much the school made from some of the activities last year." Myra's mom was president of the PTA just about every year. "I called into the system from my own computer and checked her numbers against the record. Jed, this was going on last year, too! In fact, if you figure the thief is skimming about the same percentage off everything, there's almost three thousand dollars missing, just from this year and last!"

I was sitting on my bedroom floor with the cordless phone, throwing wadded-up paper at the little basketball hoop stuck to my closet door. "So who's taking it?" I said.

"It might be more than one person. I asked my dad how these things work." Myra's dad is a lawyer, so he knows about legal and financial stuff. "He said there are always two names on any of the accounts for a public institution like a school. I asked him if one person could be stealing money without the other one knowing, and he said it's possible, especially if the second person is really gullible. But that's why—"

"Wait a minute. You told your *dad* about all this?"

"No, stupid. Why would I do that? I just asked him in general. Anyway, that's why they use both names—as a safeguard. So we may have two perpetrators."

"Two whats?"

She snorted. "Look it up, Webster."

Well, one thing for sure. Myra was back to

being a royal pain, just like I'd thought she'd be. She was so mad about the money being stolen she was back in her witch mode again. I felt homesick for the other side of her I'd seen at the mall last night. I threw another wad of paper. Two points.

"So while you were doing all this detective work," I asked, "did you happen to find out whose names are on the account?"

"Not yet. But I'll make you a bet. When we do find out, one of the names will be Mr. Halston."

My door opened and Alan walked in. "Close the door," I said. Then I said to Myra, "How do you know?"

"Because he's the principal. Don't you figure he'd have his name on any major account?"

Alan picked up a couple of my wadded-up basketballs and dunked them.

"But if it is—then he's a crook?" I asked, not sure what answer I was hoping for.

"Maybe. If somebody were taking the money *out* of the account, then he'd be a crook for sure.

But it looks like the money's disappearing before it's deposited. So maybe he doesn't know about it."

I paused a minute to let that sink in. "So whose is the other name?" I asked.

She hesitated. "Well, let's hope it's not Mr. Sloan."

"Mr. Sloan!" I gasped. "No way. Mr. Sloan's not a crook!"

Alan's mouth dropped open. "Myra thinks Mr. Sloan is the crook? Gimme the phone."

"How could you even think that, Myra?" I asked. "You were in Sloan's class, too. He's the best teacher we ever had."

"I know, Jed. That's why I hope it's not him. But think. Who's the adviser for all fund-raising events for the school?"

I didn't answer.

"So don't you think his signature would be the other one on the account?" she went on. "I mean, I hope it's not, Jed. But he's the one who takes all the money first and counts it and everything. And didn't it seem odd that he wouldn't let us check the records at the meeting the other day?"

Yeah, it *had* seemed weird. Especially since he's a computer whiz himself and probably could have called up those records in about two milliseconds. But I just couldn't believe that Mr. Sloan was involved in something shady. "So what?" I said. "Forget it. Halston, yes. Sloan, no."

I hung up.

Alan sat in my computer chair. "She's crazy," he said, his jaw set. "Mr. Sloan would be the *last* person who'd steal money."

I nodded. "You got that right."

The phone rang again. "Jed, you didn't give me a chance to finish," Myra said. "We've got a chance to catch whoever it is tomorrow."

"Why tomorrow?"

"The first order period in the PTA candy sale ended yesterday. Today my mom added up all the orders, and tomorrow she'll hand in the check. I can ask her how much it is. Then we just have to find out who enters the total in the computer. If the total's wrong, then we know that person's a crook."

"Wait a minute. How do we know—"

"Look," she interrupted impatiently. "If we hand somebody a check, we can assume he knows how much it is, right? And if that same person enters a different amount in the computer, then he's lying, right? And why would he lie? Because he stole the money! Is that clear, or should I have Mister Rogers explain it?"

"Yeah, okay. Bye." I hung up.

It really was too bad about Myra. For a minute or two the night before, she seemed almost human.

Chapter.10

On Saturday I sat on my sled at the top of the hill behind the school and watched Alan trudging toward me through the snow, dragging his inner tube. It had finally snowed the night before—about six inches—and the next morning the sun had come out. It was a perfect day for sledding. There were at least a couple dozen people on the hill, mostly kids from Livermore, but with a few younger kids and parents thrown in.

Myra's mom had turned her check in the day

before, and by that night no one had recorded it in the school's system. I thought the thief might do it on Saturday. Since it was a great day to be on the hill anyway, I figured I might as well just hang out behind the school and watch. I might catch him in the act.

"You call Myra?" I asked as Alan came up the hill, breathing hard.

He nodded, dropping his tube onto the snow and plopping down on it. "She wasn't too happy about it. Said the thief would probably wait till Monday, and we'd get cold and wet for nothing."

"Yeah, I don't guess she's into winter sports much," I said, trying to imagine Myra on ice skates.

Alan watched as a kid sledded the hill. "So what happens if the thief just calls into the system through the phone lines and enters it that way?"

"No problem," I said. "Here's why. There are a lot of outside phone lines from the computers in the media center, so kids can call into

ByteLine and stuff, right?"

"Right."

"But there's only one line for calling *in* to the school's main computer system—the line we've been using."

"Wait. How do you know that?"

"Myra found that out working in the office. Anyway, if I keep that one line busy, the thief will have to come down to school in person to enter the candy sale results. And we'll be waiting."

"Yeah," Alan said. He got up and stepped back a few steps. "Or he could just wait till Monday." He ran forward to throw himself onto the tube on his belly. He got a pretty good ride, and I headed down right behind him.

"Hey, Jed," Alan said as we trudged back up the hill. "Do you think Myra's cute?"

I couldn't believe my ears. "Did you just say what I thought you said?" I asked.

"Hey, I didn't say *I* thought she was cute. I just asked. Because last night I said something to my parents about Myra being ugly, and they looked at me weird. 'Myra Steinmetz?' they said. I said yeah, and they said, 'She's going to be a knockout when she gets older.' I told 'em they were thinking of the wrong girl, and they laughed at me. I just wondered if I was crazy or something."

"You're not crazy, but your parents are. I mean, there are lots of cute girls at school, but Myra's not one of them. She's skinny, she's uncoordinated, she—"

"Shut up," Alan mumbled. "She's here."

I looked up. There was Myra, standing at the top of the hill. She was wearing her humongous parka and ugly purple boots. "You bring a sled?" I asked, jogging the last few steps to the top.

She shook her head. "Don't have one."

"Want to use mine?"

She nodded and took it. I could tell by the way she sat on it that she hadn't done this much. I pushed her to give her a start, and she zipped down the hill.

"Did she hear you?" Alan whispered.

I shrugged. "Who cares?" I grabbed his inner

tube out of his hands and jumped on it, getting a pretty fast run down the hill. The whole way down I thought to myself, *You cared at the mall the other night.*

Myra was just sitting at the bottom on my sled when I coasted to a stop beside her. "You have to drag it back up," I said. "It only goes by itself downhill."

She looked at me. "I know that." Then we just looked at each other for a minute. "You're not exactly a movie star yourself, Jed," she said.

I had a couple of comebacks, but I shut my mouth before I said anything. Then I opened it to apologize. Then I shut it. "What are you, some kind of fish?" she said.

Now, I *really* couldn't think of anything to say. *Boy, am I an idiot,* I thought.

Myra just looked at me. Then she said, "So, are you in the system?"

"Yep. Tapped into it as soon as I got here."

"Good. That's why we're here, after all. It sure isn't because I enjoy your company."

"Geronimo!" A man's voice came from the

top of the hill, and we turned around to see Mr. Sloan leap down the hill without a sled. He landed on his stomach, and then twisted over onto his back and headed straight for us. He was going pretty fast, too. He had on a ski jacket with slippery nylon fabric. Myra got a scared look on her face and darted out of the way.

"All right!" I said when he slid to a stop. "Good one! Hey, you want to use my sled?"

"Wish I could," he said. "I saw you guys up here, and I thought, hey, why should they have all the fun? So I came out for one trip down the hill. But I really just stopped by to pick up some stuff, then I've got to head out. Got papers to grade today. What a great day, huh?" He spread his arms wide and gave a Tarzan yell.

"You're supposed to beat on your chest when you do that," I said, but my grin felt strange on my face.

"Never could get that right," he laughed. "Well, hey, I'm outta here. See you Monday." He waved at all the kids back up on the hill and trudged off through the snow toward the building.

Myra and I stood and watched him go. "Let's go back up," she said quietly.

We all three sat on Alan's inner tube and waited for something to happen. When Mr. Sloan had been inside the school about five minutes, I saw something moving on the screen. Somebody was opening the database.

"Any changes?" Alan asked.

"Shhhh."

Somebody went into the fund-raising records and opened a new file named "Candy Sale Proceeds."

"What's happening?" Myra whispered.

"Somebody's recording the candy sale proceeds. Fourth grade, $89.30. Fifth grade, $112.85. Sixth grade, $124.15. Total, $326.30. That's it. Program's closing."

Myra frowned. "That's right. Those are the right numbers." She was checking the figures against a piece of paper she had pulled out of her pocket.

Alan must have been holding his breath

because he blew a big lungful of it out in relief, and he and I both laughed. Boy, it felt great. Mr. Sloan wasn't keeping any of the money. He wasn't a thief. I mentally backed out of the program and broke the connection.

"Hey, Myra," I said. "My gosh, this isn't exactly a funeral. What's with the face? Mr. Sloan *didn't* take the money, in case you weren't paying attention." I stood up and grabbed my sled, ready to make another run down the hill.

"Doesn't it seem odd to you," Myra said, "that every fund-raising activity for the past two years, as near as we can tell, has had money skimmed off—and now, suddenly, just this one doesn't? Why's that, do you suppose?"

I shrugged. "Maybe somebody else entered the money for all the others—somebody who kept some of it for himself."

"Yeah," Alan added, "like Mr. Halston maybe."

Myra stood up, brushed herself off, and shook her head. "Doesn't seem likely. Are you still in the program?"

"Nope," I said.

"Dial back in. Check the numbers."

I stared at her.

"Just do it," she said.

"We just looked at 'em, Myra," I said. "You think they're any different now?"

She glared at me, and I sighed and called up my communications program and dialed into the system all over again.

"Call up the fund-raising records again," Myra said.

"All right, all right," I grumbled. "Okay. Candy sale proceeds. Fourth grade, $22.30. Fifth grade—"

I stopped talking. The numbers were all wrong.

"What's the total?" Myra asked quietly.

"$81.58," I said.

We all sat back down.

"The original total was over three hundred," Myra said.

"But this is crazy," I said. "We just looked at it a couple minutes ago, and it had the right numbers."

"So how could that happen, Alan?" Myra asked.

Alan thought quietly. "Well," he said finally, "there are a couple of ways. Somebody who knew what he was doing could program the system to revise the numbers by a certain percentage as the program closes. Or, of course, somebody could have re-entered the program and changed it."

"But why would anybody do that?" I said.

"Protection," Myra said.

"What?"

"He enters the right numbers, then he prints out a copy of the report with the right numbers on it, or just copies it to a disk for his file. Then he goes back in and changes the numbers. That way he's got a record that he entered the numbers correctly, and nobody can prove he's the one who changed them."

"Nobody except us," Alan said quietly.

"That's crazy!" I hissed. "We can't prove anything! *Anybody* could have changed those numbers!"

"How?" Myra asked. "Nobody else knew he'd entered them. How would they have known to change them?"

We watched Mr. Sloan leave the school and walk across the parking lot to his car. He waved. We waved back.

"Could be somebody else in the building," I said.

Myra started to say something, but then stopped.

"No other cars in the parking lot," Alan said. "Who'd your mom give the check to?" he asked Myra.

"Mr. Sloan."

"So what?" I said. I felt warm despite the chilly air. "You haven't proved anything yet. You still don't know what happened to the money. All you've got is a bunch of numbers on a school computer. The police are just going to laugh in your face."

My favorite teacher drove away. I grabbed my sled and walked home.

Chapter. 11

"Where are you going, Jed?" my mom asked.

It was after dinner that same day. She was sitting at the dining room table, papers and books spread out. She looked a little frantic and worried. It made me realize I'll be glad when she's done with her degree. Sometimes it's like I only have half a mom.

"Just out for a walk. Maybe over to Todd's."

She looked at me funny. I'd been in a strange mood since I got back from sledding with Alan and Myra, and she had asked a couple of times if I felt okay.

"Well, don't be gone long," she said, still with that look on her face. "It's getting very cold tonight. Will you be warm enough? Should you take a heavier coat? Put a hat on, Jed."

I put on a wool cap just so I wouldn't have to argue about it with her. By the time I headed out the door, though, she was chewing her lip and digging frantically through her books and didn't even see me leave, hat or not. Why would *anybody* go to school if they didn't have to?

It really *was* cold. The snow scrunched under my feet the way it does when the temperature's down near zero. The air was doing funny things with the lights, and smoke from chimneys was going straight out to the side instead of up. Weird.

I tromped along toward Antelope Park for no particular reason. I wasn't really thinking about where I was going. I had so many thoughts swirling around in my head I couldn't catch one of them long enough to really think about it.

There had to be some other explanation. Mr. Sloan couldn't be the thief. I felt like I was failing him because I couldn't figure out what was really going on. I knew if I sat down with Alan and Myra we'd be able to think better together, but I didn't trust them right now. I felt like they already believed Mr. Sloan was guilty.

Myra. It was so weird! I mean, she's just this tall, skinny girl with a tongue that can kill a person, right? But I found myself thinking about her a lot, and remembering how she looked that night at the mall, and feeling like I was the most important person in the world to her at that moment, and wishing I could make that moment come back.

I was halfway through the park to the children's zoo by this time, but I turned around and started walking back the way I came. My ears and toes hurt, I was so cold. It even hurt to breathe. There was a gas station and convenience store back on the corner, and I headed for it. I had to get into some warm air.

This whole computer-in-my-head thing—it had seemed so great at first, but what could I do with it? Cheat. Except that hadn't turned out to be such a great idea, because Alan and Myra caught me, and now how was I gonna get the grades I needed? If my dad took my computer away…

And then this whole thing with the money being stolen. It made me wish none of this had ever happened and I was just Jed Vanderlaan with a plain old human brain again.

I was in pain by the time I got to the convenience store. I walked in and stomped my feet a few times. Then I took off my mittens and my hat to let the warm air get to me. I had a couple of bucks in my pocket. I thought maybe I'd get some hot chocolate and a donut or something.

"Hey, Jed, my man!" It was Mr. Sloan, just coming through the door behind me. He was bundled up in a down parka, with a knit cap under the hood. He grinned. "You look like you're in never-never land, pal. I was out there gassing up my car, and you trudged on past, dead to the world. Didn't even see me. Why are you out freezing your tail anyway?" He grabbed a gallon of milk and gave the clerk a credit card. "Twelve bucks for the gas," he said, then turned back to me. "So, your parents finally kick you out, or what?"

I wanted to grin and tease him back, like I usually did, but it just wouldn't come. He looked at me funny, then signed the slip, pulled his gloves back on, picked up his milk, and motioned with his head for me to follow him outside.

"Now," he said, crunching through the icy snow toward his car, "to what do we owe this serious expression?"

If I had thought about this ahead of time, I would have been too scared to say anything. But there we were, and I just cleared my throat and blurted it out, with lips so numb I wasn't sure he could understand me. "Suppose, uh...," I stumbled, "suppose you had this friend. And this friend was doing something really wrong, and you found out about it. Just suppose. Or at least you *thought* this friend was doing something wrong, but you weren't sure. And you didn't want to say anything about it or else you'd get this friend in trouble, and you didn't want to do that, because this was a really good friend. But then, it wouldn't be fair to other people if you let what this person was doing just go on happening." I wasn't saying this very well. "You know what I mean so far?"

He put the milk into his car and then stood there and studied me. "I think so," he said. "Go on."

I cleared my throat again. "So what I need to know is, what should you do? If you knew about something like this. Tell and get your friend in trouble? Or what?"

He looked out into the street for a few seconds. There weren't many cars out on a night like this. "This something bad that this person is doing," he said. "Is it something like cheating on tests?"

"Sort of," I said. "Well, no. Worse. Like

breaking the law. Like a crime. Like stealing something."

He was quiet for a while. Then he said, "And you're afraid your friend will go to juvenile hall or something like that?"

"Well," I said, "not juvenile hall. This person is a grown-up. So it's more like jail."

He turned slowly back and looked at me, his expression thoughtful. I couldn't look at his face so I looked at his feet. He closed the car door slowly and then leaned against the car and stood there looking down, stroking his chin with his gloved hand.

I waited, stepping from one foot to the other. My face had started to hurt again, and I knew I couldn't stand there much longer. "And is it money that this friend is stealing?" he asked quietly.

I chipped away at some ice with the toe of my boot. I nodded.

"And maybe this friend—this grown-up friend—is stealing this money—well, let's say from needy people. Is that right?"

I wished I was anywhere but where I was. I nodded again, looking at my mittens.

He was quiet for a long time. A police car went by, and we both watched it go. Then he looked slowly back toward me. "Well, Jed, sounds like you've got a tough decision to make," he said quietly. "And you're asking me to make it for you. Wish I could, my friend. But you've got to do what *you* think is right."

I still couldn't look at his eyes. I glanced up once, and he was looking at me. I looked back down. "If you decided to tell," I said, "would you, uh, would you tell the person before you told the police? To kind of warn them?" I looked at him again. "Since it's a friend."

He smiled sadly, his breath coming out in a thick white cloud. "Well, I guess that is something a friend would do," he said, nodding. "Although it sounds like this person hasn't been much of a friend to you."

That almost made me cry. "Oh, yes," I said. "Yes, he has."

Then he shook his head, opened his car

door, and climbed in. He shut the door, but rolled the window down. "Don't stay out here too long, Jed. This cold is brutal."

I was halfway back to the store before I remembered to turn around and say, "Goodnight, Mr. Sloan."

He was just sitting there, his window down, watching me go. "Good-bye, Jed," he said quietly. "And thanks."

The next Wednesday morning, before the bell rang, Myra and Alan and I stood in the hallway outside Mr. Sloan's room. A red-headed girl who didn't look much older than a teenager came rushing down the hall with a nervous look on her face and hurried through Mr. Sloan's door.

None of us said anything for a few seconds, and then Alan said, "Okay, third day in a row he's had a substitute."

"Maybe he really is sick," I said.

"Or maybe he left town because he didn't want to be arrested, Jed," Myra said quietly. "I know you don't want to believe that, but what are we supposed to believe? You tell him we know, and then he disappears."

We were already late for class, but we had something more important on our minds. We each got a drink from the fountain nearby and then just stood for a minute.

"So do we go to the police?" Alan asked at last. "I mean, we did discover a crime."

I looked at Myra. "Why can't we just talk to him first? We could give him a chance to pay all the money back."

"Is that what you'd do if it was Mr. Halston?" Myra asked.

"It wasn't Mr. Halston," I said through clenched teeth. "It was Mr. Sloan! The best teacher we ever had." I backed away from them, toward our classroom. Right then, I hated them both. "I can't believe you guys," I said. "This is Mr. Sloan!"

Chapter. 12

Dad had gone to the hospital to make his rounds on Saturday afternoon, and Mom was at the university library. I was home by myself watching a video. Suddenly somebody started pounding on the front door and I heard Alan yell, "Jed! Open up!"

Alan and Myra rushed in, throwing off coats and hats and scarves, as soon as I opened the door. "It wasn't Mr. Sloan!" Alan said excitedly.

"Alan!" Myra scolded. "We don't know that! Stop saying that!"

"Wait—it wasn't Mr. Sloan? What are you talking about?" I said.

"Be quiet, Alan," Myra commanded. "Let me explain. Yesterday my mom gave another check for candy sales to Mr. Halston. This morning, just out of curiosity, I dialed into the school's computer system to check the records."

"And the amounts entered in the fund-raising records were wrong!" Alan interrupted. "Mr. Sloan's gone—that means somebody else entered the wrong numbers! So it wasn't Mr. Sloan, right?"

"Alan, just think for a minute," Myra said, surprisingly patient. "You yourself said somebody could have revised the program to change the figures automatically when the program closes. That somebody could have been Mr. Sloan. And besides, we don't know whether Mr. Sloan's still gone. He might have come back. And even if there is someone else—well, I said way back in the beginning it might take two people to pull this off. Mr. Sloan might still be involved. We just don't know. So stop saying that. You'll just make it worse."

For once, I agreed with Myra. "I want to see this for myself," I said, mentally dialing into the school's system.

"Listen," Myra said. "I was thinking about it on the way over. Suppose there *are* two thieves. We can try to talk Mr. Sloan—if he comes back—into testifying against the other guy. That way he might get a lighter sentence."

I wasn't getting anything. I dialed the number again.

"You think he'd do it?" Alan asked. "Wouldn't that be kind of like being a traitor or something?"

"I'm trying to get into the system," I said. "I can't get through."

"Busy signal?" Myra asked.

"No busy signal," I said, "no dial tone, no ringing—nothing."

We looked at each other.

"Try it again," Myra said.

"I already tried it twice." But I tried it again. "Nothing."

"Hey," Alan said, "suppose there is another guy. Suppose he's getting worried because Mr. Sloan's gone. Could he be dumping the data right now—destroying the evidence?"

We looked at each other for a second or two, and then Myra slapped the side of her head. "Idiots!" she said. "We are idiots! Why didn't we print it out?"

We jumped up and grabbed our coats. I hopped on one foot out the door as I pulled on my second boot. Alan and Myra were right behind me.

We raced down the first block, but then we had to slow down to a jog. It had stayed cold through the week, and there were a couple inches of new snow, so it was slow going. Finally we jogged up to the side of the school. There were no cars in the lot.

"There's nobody here," Myra said. "Try dialing in again."

I did. "Still nothing," I said.

"Maybe he disconnected the system," Alan said. "Let's go around to the front and look into the office through the windows."

What we saw when we got there was incredible! There was black smoke—lots of it—rising from the windows.

"It's a fire!" Myra said. "The building's on fire! Alan, run over to that house and call 911!"

Alan ran off. My mind was racing a mile a minute. Suddenly, it focused on the obvious. "The computers!" I yelled. We ran up to the office windows but all we could see inside was smoke. We ran to the front doors, but they were locked. We heard fire alarms going crazy inside.

"Break the glass!" Myra said. "We can reach through and open the door from the inside." She punched the glass with her mittened fist, but the door barely rattled.

"They must use really thick glass on these doors," I said. "We need a rock or a hammer or something." I looked around. There was nothing but snow and chunks of ice. I heard voices and looked out toward the street. Three men were running toward the school. One of them was Tony Palmiero's dad. They must have seen the smoke. "We need to break this glass so we can get in!" I yelled.

"Is somebody in there?" one of them yelled back.

"I don't think so," I said.

Tony's dad puffed as he ran up beside us, a crowbar in his hand. I could hear the sirens from the fire trucks. "Stand back, kids," he said. He swung the crowbar awkwardly, but the glass broke. It took him a minute or two to clear it out of the way so that he could reach through and pull the inside lever to open the door. He and the other men rushed in. "Where's the extinguisher?" one yelled.

Myra and I tried to follow them in, but one of the men saw us and held up a hand. "Whoa! You kids stay out—and stay far away from the building. Go on! Move!" He pushed us roughly out the door.

Sirens wailing, the fire trucks pulled into the driveway and parked where the school buses usually did in the big curving drive. Suddenly, men in slick, long black coats were everywhere, and they weren't happy to see us close to the school. "Back to the sidewalk, kids!" one yelled. "Now! And stay there!"

We dragged ourselves up to the climbing tower, which was made of logs and stood on a hill above the action, about level with the school's roof. Alan joined us, and the three of us kicked the snow off one of the logs and then sat hunched up in the cold, watching the fire fighters run back and forth, yelling. They broke out all the windows near the office, and smoke poured out. Soon water was spraying everywhere from fire hoses. It froze into huge icicles on the outside of the school.

"Gosh," Alan said finally. "You don't suppose somebody set this fire on purpose, do you?"

"Whatever gave you that idea?" Myra mumbled, sarcastically.

I gathered up some snow near my feet and rolled it into a snowball, which I tossed toward the school. We kept watching for another fifteen minutes or so. Then things seemed to slow down. The fire fighters only had a couple of hoses still going, and a lot of the men just seemed to be standing around. We could hear a few snatches of conversation: "started in the office," "most of the damage confined to the one room," stuff like that.

"Here come some more cops," Alan said. Two cop cars had shown up about the same time as the fire trucks, but a couple more pulled up now and parked just below us. The front doors opened and the officers climbed slowly out.

Myra sucked her breath in sharply. "Oh, no," she said.

"What?" I said.

She pointed. "Check out the back seat."

We looked. Sitting in the back seat of the nearest patrol car, looking unshaven and mussed and miserable, was Mr. Sloan.

Stunned, I just stared, unable to think. The officer who'd been driving the car Mr. Sloan was in stood talking to the fire chief. They called over Tony's dad and the other men who'd arrived at the fire right after us and asked them some questions. The men talked for a while, then looked around, spotted us, and pointed.

The police officer walked to the bottom of the hill below us. "Would you kids come down here for a minute, please?" he asked.

We got down from the tower and walked down the hill.

"You kids were the first to get here?" the police officer said.

We nodded.

"Did you spot anything unusual—somebody in the parking lot, any sign that somebody had been in the school, anything like that?"

We shook our heads. "We just saw the smoke coming out of the windows," I said.

He looked disappointed. "Well, give us your names and phone numbers in case we have any other questions."

So we did. Then I took a chance. "Uh, you have one of my teachers in your police car," I said. "Did he get hurt in the fire?"

The officer looked at me sharply. "No, he wasn't hurt," he said. "Thanks for your help." And that was it.

Alan headed toward home. Myra and I went back to the hill and climbed up on the log tower again. The sun was almost down and it was getting pretty cold, but we sat and waited until the last of the fire fighters had finished up and all the trucks were gone.

"Well," I said, standing up, "nothing we can do around here."

"Hey, kids," said a wheezy voice.

We turned around to see a man stepping carefully through the snow toward us in a bright ski parka that looked like it just came off the rack. He had on leather shoes and kept slipping in the snow.

It was Mr. Garfield, the computer technician.

Chapter. 13

"Glad you kids were around to help me out," Mr. Garfield said. We had followed him down the hill to the walkway by the school's front doors. He lifted the yellow police tape out of the way, walked underneath it, and then held it up for us to follow. He snorted when he saw us hesitate. "Don't worry," he said. "The cops already said it was okay."

He crunched across the broken glass to the front door, then put his shoulder to the door to move it out of the way. Everything was icing up from all the water that had been sprayed at the school. We followed him into the entryway. What a mess. The fire fighters had knocked stuff off the wall. They'd pulled half-burned stuff out of the office and just left it anywhere. Myra and I looked at each other and shook our heads. It made my stomach hurt. Even if you hate school, it's still *your* school, you know?

"What we got to do is, we got to load the damaged computer gear into my van so I can take it back to the shop. You guys get started moving this junk out of the way, and I'll go pull my van up. This shouldn't take long." Then he clomped back out the door, glass and ice crackling under his feet.

We moved slowly into the office. It was a disaster area. Everything was blackened from the smoke. The fire fighters had tipped desks over, and file cabinet drawers were scattered around the room. We didn't know where to start.

"Kind of strange, don't you think?" Myra said in a low voice.

"What's strange?" I said.

"That he got here so fast. And that he's in such a hurry to get these computers back down to the shop to be worked on. It's late. And it's Saturday. Nobody's going to work on them tonight."

We started grabbing anything small enough to drag or carry and hauled it out into the hallway. A couple of minutes later, Mr. Garfield came down the hall from the direction of the utility doors. "I just called Mr. Halston," he said. "He's on his way down, but he asked us to start carrying a few of these files down into storage in the basement. Let me show you." He loaded us up with an armload each of files. "Come on. Down this way."

Down the hallway we all went, and then through a door he had to unlock that went to the basement. I'd never been in the basement at Livermore before that day. I had no idea what was kept down there. It was cold, that was for sure. It was like going down the stairs into a huge refrigerator. The light bulbs were bare, and there was gritty dirt under our feet.

The stairway ended in a large open area with lots of dusty old equipment and furniture stacked around—tables, old movie projectors, bookcases. *This must be where old school stuff comes to die,* I thought.

"In here," Mr. Garfield said, squeezing between a couple of huge cabinets. We followed. He pushed open a door and turned on a light.

The room we stepped into looked like an old office. "On that desk over there," Mr. Garfield said, pointing.

I dumped the files on the desk and rubbed my sore arms. Just as Myra was moving up to the desk to drop her stuff, I heard the door close and the lock click. I turned around and saw nothing but the unpainted, dusty inside of the door. "Hey!" I yelled. "Let us out!"

"Yeah, right," Mr. Garfield's voice came back, muffled by the door. "Fat chance."

I grabbed the knob and rattled it.

"Why'd you lock us in here?" Myra said, sounding more angry than scared.

"Because you snoops like to stick your noses

in where you don't belong, that's why," Mr. Garfield said. "I mean, you guys—" We heard him rustling around with something, then heard a cigarette lighter flick on followed by a puff of his breath. "You must really think I'm dumb or something, you know that?" The stink of his cigarette smoke crept under the door. "You think I can't trace calls that come into your school's system? All I got to do is push a button. I set it up that way. By the way, I got *two* phone lines into the school, not just one. Nobody knows about the second line but me. I can follow your trail every time you call into the school's system here. I know who's calling and what file you're into. Idiots."

Myra gasped all of a sudden and sat down in a dusty old desk chair. "He's right," she said quietly. "I am an idiot. I just remembered. Mr. Halston isn't even in town. My mom called him last week to ask him to attend a PTA meeting tonight, and he said he'd be at a principals conference in Seattle. So Mr. Garfield *couldn't* have called him. I should have known he was lying."

"So it wasn't Mr. Sloan after all," I whispered.

Mr. Garfield whapped the door, hard. "Stop whispering in there!" Then we heard him take a deep drag and twist his shoe on his cigarette butt. "Anyway, I got a problem now. I don't know how much you've figured out from all your calls into the system, but it must be plenty, or you wouldn't have kept checking. If I'd just left you alone, you might have gone straight to the police before I could get out of here with my money."

"So get your money and catch a plane somewhere," Myra said. "Leave us here. By the time somebody lets us out, you'll be gone."

Mr. Garfield chuckled, coughing a little. "Nice try. But the money's not just sitting in a suitcase somewhere. I've got it stashed electronically in clean accounts nobody can trace back to me. It'll take me a while to access it all, transfer it to where I can get to it—probably twenty-four hours. And by morning, this place will be jumping with insurance adjusters and everybody else. Some of 'em may even turn up tonight yet. So that's my problem."

We heard him light another cigarette. It seemed like hours before he spoke again. Finally he said, "You kids sit tight. I'll be back."

We heard his footsteps on the stairs. Then a door banged shut.

Myra was still sitting in the dusty chair. Her hands were shaking a little. She hugged herself, and I don't think it was because of the cold.

"Well, he's got us pretty much where he wants us," I said, my voice sounding weird. I kept seeing this image of the two of us lying dead someplace, X's over our eyes like in some old cartoon. I shook my head, hard. "Come on," I said. "We've got to find a way out."

Myra jumped up from the chair, and then turned around and started pulling open drawers in the desk beside her. "You're right," she said. "There's got to be some way out."

"But he won't be gone long," I said, looking all around the room for something—anything— that might help us. "Whatever we're going to do, we'd better do it soon."

"He hasn't said anything about Alan," Myra said, stretching to look behind the desk. "Maybe he doesn't know about him. Whenever we called into the system, we always did it from your house or my house. Hey," she said, pulling a telephone book out of a desk drawer. "I suppose it's too much to ask that there be a phone in here somewhere."

I stopped moving boxes and looked up at her. "What did you say?"

She was leaning across the desk to look behind the file cabinet. "A phone. We could call the police."

I grinned. "A phone. Yeah, we got a phone. Just leave me alone for a minute," I said. I closed my eyes, opened my ByteLine software, and chose "Sign On." After a few seconds the main ByteLine screen came up, and I chose "Face to Face," where all the discussion rooms are.

"ByteLine?" Myra asked.

I nodded, eyes still closed.

"Try to find Alan," she suggested.

Alan probably hadn't been home very long. It didn't seem likely he would have signed on to ByteLine yet. From the main Face to Face menu, I chose Hacker's Forum. You can get a list of everybody who's in the room at that moment, and I called up that list. Rats. No "Waterboy." That was Alan's screen name. I scrolled down the list, looking for any name I recognized, anybody I'd talked to before—aha! There was a good one—GIBill, a guy who lived in Grand Island. I clicked back into the discussion room and typed in:

Jedediah: GIBill GIBill EMERGENCY. NEED YOU RIGHT NOW.

Mentally I hit the return key to send the message. I got a response in seconds.

GIBill: Hey, Jedediah. Haven't heard from you in a while. What's up?

Jedediah: Emergency, emergency. GIBill, call Alan Ward in Lincoln at 555-4036. Tell him to call into this room. HURRY.

There was a short pause, and then the

message came.

GIBill: Is this a joke, Jedediah? What's the emergency?

Jedediah: No joke, GIBill. Please hurry. Life and death. PLEASE!

His answer came back quickly.

GIBill: OK. Signing off to call Alan.

"What's happening?" Myra asked.

"Alan hadn't signed on," I explained. "I asked somebody else to call him and get him on there quick."

She nodded, thinking that over. GIBill must have rushed, because before she could even answer, I saw Alan's message click on at the bottom of the screen:

Waterboy: Here I am. What's going on?

Jedediah: Alan, it's Jed. Quick, call 911. Garfield locked me and Myra in the school basement. He's the thief. Don't ask questions.

DO IT.

We waited a few minutes, expecting to hear Garfield open the door any second. There were lots of comments from the other people in the room, most of them angry because they thought I was just teasing, but I ignored them—all except the one from GIBill, who wanted to know if I was okay. I told him I was—so far. Finally Alan came back on.

Waterboy: Police on other line. Cars on way to school.

Alan was online so often that his parents had put in a second phone line just for the computer. That really came in handy now. He could talk to the police on the phone at the same time he watched his screen.

I was just starting to key in a reply when the door banged open and Garfield reached in, grabbed Myra's arm, and yanked her through. She screamed, but I was too slow to think of trying to pull her back, and then the door slammed again. "I'll be back for you in a few minutes," Garfield yelled. "Just cooperate and nobody gets hurt. If you give me a hard time when I come back, I'll hurt your friend here. It's that simple."

I felt my heart drop. I only hoped the cops could make it in time.

Five minutes later, Myra and I were both sitting on the floor in the back of Mr. Garfield's black van. He'd taken the seats out. Our feet were tied at the ankles, and our hands were tied behind our backs. I'd sent another message while I was waiting downstairs, telling Alan to get the cops to hurry. As Garfield had brought me out to the van, there'd been just enough light that I'd seen what I needed to see: the van's license plate, HGR 463.

He climbed into the driver's seat and started the engine. "Okay, you're supposed to be such smart kids," he said, "so I'm sure I don't have to tell you not to try anything—such as hollering at a police car." He opened the glove compartment, took something out, and held it up for us to see. It was dark, so it took a minute to recognize what was in his hand. When I did, I felt real cold all of a sudden.

"He's got a gun," Myra whispered.

"That's right, little girl," Garfield said. "A gun. And I know how to use it. Just in case you kids aren't as smart as you're supposed to be."

Mr. Garfield was definitely a bad guy. A nutso bad guy.

He tucked the gun into his coat pocket and drove across the school parking lot with his lights off. He turned them on just before he pulled out onto the street and turned right toward Capital Parkway. As we drove off down the street, I looked back at the school and saw two cop cars pull up into the bus drive in front, red and blue lights flashing.

Chapter.14

"Oh, man," Mr. Garfield said, glancing in his rearview mirror. "How in the—oh, wait. Of course. Sloan."

We looked at each other. "Mr. Sloan?" Myra asked.

Mr. Garfield accelerated. Then he chuckled. "Yeah. Your Mr. Sloan. Teacher of the Year. He's a crook."

"*You're* the crook," I said, confused. "You already admitted it."

He laughed. It was the kind of laugh that sent

chills down my spine. "You have no idea. Listen," he said, "do you know how many schools there are in this school district? Twenty-seven. And I'm the computer consultant for every one of 'em. Do you have any idea how much money I've been able to, let's say, 'redirect' over the last five years?"

It's like he was bragging about it or something. How could anyone brag about being a crook?

"And when you control the computer systems, my friends, nobody even knows the money is missing. Because the holes close up by themselves. I designed it that way." He laughed that crazy laugh again as he turned north onto Capital Parkway.

"You know," Myra said, her voice shaking, "I don't think you should be telling us all this."

He just laughed. "Hey, how many chances do I get—"

"No, I mean I *really* don't think you should be telling us all this," she insisted.

But I had to know. "What does Mr. Sloan have to do with it, then?" I asked.

I heard Myra sigh nervously.

"Sloan came to me last spring and said he wanted a piece of the action. Just at Livermore. But I'm telling you, there's something wacko about that guy. I think he's the one who called the cops. Maybe he freaked. Or maybe he thinks he can pin the whole thing on me this way."

My stomach dropped. "I don't believe you," I said.

Mr. Garfield shook his head. "What is it about that guy? I mean, everybody acts like he's some saint or something. I'm telling you the guy's a crook. He comes up to me one night when we're both at the school working late, and says he knows what I'm up to and he'll blow the whistle if I don't cut him in. So I cut him in, just to keep him quiet. Big deal. Then he disappears a few days ago, and I start to worry. I mean, maybe he's having a conscience attack or something. So I count up what I've got stashed away and decide it's time to destroy the evidence and split."

"So *you* set the school on fire!" I spluttered. "But why?"

I heard Myra whisper frantically, "Don't ask! Don't ask him anything!" but I ignored her and went on.

"You stole from twenty-seven different schools, you said. They can use the computer files from the others as evidence against you."

"No, they can't," he said. "I told you I designed the system, right? So it leaves no clues. There's no trail to follow."

"Wait—then why burn Livermore?" I said.

"Because Sloan changed the system."

"What?"

"He changed the system to leave the gates open. Basically, he altered my programs to show where the money was going. That was the one school in the district whose computer files could convict me—the one system that left a trail to follow. Somebody discovers the crime, and at Livermore all signs point to me, not him. He's in the clear. Besides, that way he's got something over me."

We both slumped against the van walls. Now Mr. Sloan wasn't just a crook. He was a smart and devious crook who would turn on his partner to protect himself. I wanted to throw up.

I looked around. We were almost downtown. Alan was getting frantic, sending one message after another:

Waterboy: Jed, Jed, where are you? Police have several cars searching. Jed, come in. Police want to know how you're sending messages. What should I say?

I could just see Alan, sitting there with a frantic look on his face, the phone tucked against his shoulder so he could talk to the police and type at the same time. I mentally keyed in a response and sent it:

Jedediah: Garfield taking us north on Capital Parkway in black Dodge van HGR 463. Make something up to tell police.

I opened my eyes. We were almost up to the capitol building already—a big, tall building with a golden dome. But Garfield took 17th Street north up to O Street and turned west. I keyed in another message:

Jedediah: Heading west on O St. HGR 463. Just passing 14th St.

Garfield pulled off O Street just before the bridge over the railroad switching yard and drove down toward the post office, next to the railroad tracks. He parked at the post office, facing the O Street bridge, and turned his lights off but left the engine running. "Now let's make sure we're not being followed," he muttered.

I shifted, trying to get less uncomfortable. My arms were getting sore from being held behind my back, my hands were smushed against the side of the van, and my legs were stiff. My heart was racing.

Jedediah: Parked at post office next to switching yard. Lights out. Watching for cop cars on O Street bridge.

Just as I sent the message, a patrol car zoomed across the bridge toward the west—obviously in a hurry, but no lights flashing. Maybe the cops were looking for us, but didn't want to let Garfield see them coming. Another cop car came across the bridge toward the east.

Garfield shook his head. "How on earth…" He looked back at us. "Anything you juvenile delinquents want to tell me about these cops?" he asked. He seemed really nervous. He couldn't stop moving and twitching.

We didn't answer. We didn't dare.

"No?" he said. "I bet a hundred bucks you know something about this that I don't."

You got that right, I thought.

He drove out of the parking lot and turned his lights back on. He pulled back out to O Street. "I'm gonna try something," he said thoughtfully. He crossed the bridge, then pulled off O Street into another parking lot. He turned his lights out again. Right at the base of the bridge, there was a hill almost as high as the bridge itself. He pulled up there, his tires slipping a little in the snow, and then just sat and waited, engine running. Across the railroad switching yard, we could see the post office.

I felt Myra's feet on top of mine. I was about

to move my feet away until I looked at her. In the dim light from the streetlights over the bridge, I saw that her cheeks were wet. I leaned toward her. "We'll be okay," I whispered, even though I wasn't all that sure I was telling her the truth.

Myra shook her head. "He'll kill us," she whispered back, her mouth twisted.

I felt a sharp, icy pain shoot down my back. "No he won't."

She nodded. "He will. He told us everything. He can't let us go now."

"Shut up back there!" Garfield yelled.

I shook my head at her and leaned back. But I was as scared as she was. What if she was right?

Thirty seconds later, three cop cars zipped into the post office parking lot, lights flashing.

"They knew!" Garfield sputtered. "They knew where we were! It's like they bugged my car or something! That's it, man. I'm out of here." The van slipped almost sideways down the hill. Mr. Garfield whipped out onto O Street again, turned his lights on, and sped west.

Alan sent another message.

Waterboy: Jed where are you?

Jedediah: Heading west on O, west of railroad yard.

I sent the message and then watched behind us to see how long it would take. Within a minute, Mr. Garfield hit the brakes. "What the…" I twisted my head around. He was leaning forward, peering into the distance. I saw what he was looking at—red and blue flashers. It looked like a roadblock. "How did they…" He didn't seem capable of finishing a sentence. "Oh, great," he muttered, looking up into the rearview mirror. We looked out the back—more flashers, approaching fast. Garfield hit the gas so hard we lost our balance and tumbled down. I hit my head on Myra's feet. By the time I could sit up again, the van was speeding south. I wasn't sure what street we were on, so I took a guess.

Jedediah: Heading south on 48th.

Turned out I was wrong. We were on 40th. But it didn't matter by that time because Alan had responded:

Waterboy: Police say they can

see you.

A minute or two later, Myra gave me a hard kick in the ankle and then motioned with her head to look out the window on her side of the van. I lowered my head and looked out and saw a light in the sky, a bright light that swung around like a huge spotlight.

It was a helicopter.

Garfield took a hard left on Van Dorn, fishtailing around so bad I thought he was going off the road. But that bright light hit us and stayed with us, even when he cut south on Coddington, and I knew he'd never get away.

What I didn't know was what he'd do with us.

Garfield was concentrating so hard on driving and watching his mirrors that he didn't even see the helicopter until it swung low across the road in front of us—obviously just to let him know the game was up so he'd pull over.

It didn't work. He just slapped the steering wheel, hard. "I don't believe it," he moaned. Then he cut the wheel sharply and headed into the east entrance of Pioneer Park.

Chapter. 15

Mr. Garfield whipped past the buffalo statue and the pine grove and headed for the zoo.

Pioneer Park is this giant park out in the middle of nowhere, surrounded by woods and farms. And the zoo in the park isn't a lions-and-tigers-type zoo. It's this huge series of big outdoor pens with animals like elk and buffalo and antelope in them. Most of them stay out there year-round. We whipped past the pens and pulled up to the turnaround at the end of the road. I could see some of the animals huddled in their shelters as the van's headlights swept in an arc across the wide pens. Mr. Garfield braked to a stop, his tires sliding on the snowy pavement. Even over the idling of the engine, I could hear sirens. Looking back, I saw red and blue flashers weaving in and out through the trees. *He's had it,* I thought. *End of the line. No place to go but right back toward the cops.*

The helicopter made one more pass in front of us, but not very low because there were a lot of trees growing in the animals' pens. I could hear a voice on some kind of loudspeaker saying something.

Mr. Garfield was breathing so hard now he was almost panting. "This isn't good," he gasped. "This isn't good at all."

Then I got another message from Alan.

Waterboy: Jed, what's happening?

I had just started to key in an answer when Garfield punched the gas pedal again and cut the wheel hard, sending Myra and me rolling around in the back. I struggled back up again just in time to see him swerve into the service road right between the burro and buffalo pens— a service road that had a metal gate across it.

Crash! The van broke through. I could hear the rough metal edges scraping along the length of the van. Then we were sliding down the unplowed snowy road. We shot past the end of the pens and Mr. Garfield cut the wheel left, out into an open field. Was there a road back here he knew about? Was he just panicking? Now that we were so close to being rescued, would we die in a crash? The helicopter swooped low in front of us, so low a kid could have jumped up and—

Wham! The car hit something and stopped dead. We slammed forward and hit the backs of the front seats. It felt like my ear was broken. I was just glad it wasn't my nose. Myra screamed.

I squirmed around and pushed myself up. There was snow all over the windshield, but I could see a white shape slanting in front of us. The wind had built up a snowdrift across the field. And we were in it.

The van had stalled. Mr. Garfield, swearing

under his breath, started it up again and tried to back out of the drift, but the front tires were buried deep. He rocked the van back and forth, going from reverse to drive and back again, but we were stuck good.

He *really* started swearing then. He threw open his door, grabbed a little shovel from under the seat, and started digging around the front left tire. He had left the headlights on. Since the door was still open, the overhead light was on, too. I could see Myra. Her hair looked like somebody had taken an eggbeater to it. And her face looked white and pale. But it was her eyes that really got to me. They were flitting here and there, making her look like an animal caught in a trap.

Suddenly the chopper's spotlight hit us, and it was so weird, just like a scene from some sci-fi movie with a spaceship and everything. That *whock whock whock whock* and that bright light, and Mr. Garfield jumping up like a lunatic and turning all around, snow flying off his shovel, when that loudspeaker voice came out of the sky,

"Stay where you are! Put your hands up! You are under arrest!"

That couldn't have sounded better if it had been angels! I cheered, I really did. Loud.

"Shut up in there!" Garfield yelled. "Shut up!" And he ran around to the other side of the car and started digging again, like a madman.

The voice came again. "You are under arrest! Put your hands in the air! I repeat, you are under arrest."

Headlights swept across the van from behind, and I turned around to watch the cop cars pull out into the field behind us and fan out and stop, their headlights on the van—one, two, three, four, five of them, flashers going like a pinball machine.

Then another message came from Alan.

Waterboy: Jed, are you OK? WHAT'S GOING ON?

I sent back an answer I knew would drive him crazy, but I didn't want to take my mind off what was happening:

Jedediah: Hold on.

Then I turned down the brightness so I couldn't even see the screen.

The helicopter landed on the other side of us. Garfield threw down his shovel and pulled his gun out of his coat pocket. "Stay where you are!" he yelled, his voice high and crazy. "I've got the kids in the van and I've got a gun!"

We didn't need to be reminded of that. In fact, we ducked for a few seconds, but I couldn't see anything so I slowly poked my head just high enough to get my eyes above the bottoms of the windows. All I saw were headlights, but I've watched enough TV cop shows to be able to imagine the car doors all open and the cops crouching behind them, guns drawn.

Then a voice came over a bullhorn from the cars, just like on TV. "Looks like you're stuck, Garfield. Drop the gun and let the kids go."

Garfield's answer was to point the gun at the car. We ducked again. "You want me to shoot one of these kids just so you know I'm serious?" Right then he sounded crazy enough to do it. Myra's words echoed in my mind: *He'll kill us.*

"All right, all right!" the bullhorn voice said. "Just relax. Don't do anything stupid. Think about it, Garfield. Where you gonna go? Your van's stuck, and anyway we can't let you take the kids hostage."

"They're already my hostages!" he yelled. And suddenly the side door whipped open and he reached in and grabbed Myra by the shoulder. "No funny stuff," he hissed, looking at each of us. He pulled Myra out. Her feet were still tied, so she stumbled in the snow, trying to hop beside him as he dragged her toward the back of the van. "Take a look!" Mr. Garfield yelled.

"Just take it easy," the bullhorn voice yelled back. "Nobody has to get hurt here."

"That's up to you, pal!" Garfield yelled. His voice had a real edge to it now, like he was about to start screaming. *This guy really is nuts*, I thought. "Because I'll kill this girl, I swear I will!" he hollered. Myra looked even whiter than she had before. Even as cold as it was, Garfield was sweating really badly. His whole face was wet.

He just stood there panting and sweating for

a minute, and then he yelled into the night: "Okay, listen up! I want another car, a four-wheel drive. I want a bag of food—lots of it. And I want ten thousand bucks in small bills. Either I get all that in a half-hour, or this girl dies!"

"Don't do this, Garfield. Give us an hour," the bullhorn voice said. "We can't get all that in a half-hour. We—"

"You've got a half-hour!" Garfield screamed. He shook his head, hard, probably to clear the sweat out of his eyes.

"You know this isn't gonna work, Garfield. Drop the gun and let the kids go."

Garfield's answer was to bring the gun right up to Myra's head. She looked ready to faint.

I couldn't take it anymore so I looked away. As I did, I felt my eyes go all watery.

"All right, all right!" the bullhorn voice said. "We'll get the stuff you asked for. It'll take us an hour, though. So just relax, don't do anything stupid."

"You have twenty-five minutes, and then I

start shooting!"

"You can't take the kids," the voice said. "You can take one of us. We'll exchange hostages."

"No way," Garfield said. I looked up again and saw Garfield shake his head, then move his gun away from Myra's head to wipe his eyes with the sleeve of his jacket—and Myra dropped. As soon as she saw the gun move away from her head, she just disappeared, straight down.

And then everything happened at once.

Garfield yelled, "Hey!" and started to kneel down to get her. Then he seemed to remember he was surrounded by armed police and stood again and raised his gun. Suddenly a blur crashed into him from behind, knocking him down. He was too close to the van for me to see, but I did see the rush of uniformed men, each of them holding a gun, and two of them jumped down beside the van, down where Garfield had landed. There were several thumps against the side of the van as they struggled, and then a tall police officer jumped up and yelled back down at the ground, "All right! Put your hands on the back of your head and don't move! You're under arrest. You have the right to remain silent…"

Chapter. 16

"Can I get any of you anything else?" the officer asked. "Candy bar? Our menu's kind of limited, but…"

It was around ten o'clock that night, and we were all sitting around a big table in a room at the police station—Alan, Myra, me, and all our parents. Myra's parents were still dressed up in their fancy clothes from some concert or something they'd been to. "I think we're fine," her mom said, reaching up to take off her dangly diamond earrings. "Unless you kids…"

We shook our heads. The three of us had cups of hot chocolate. Our parents had coffee. We'd been there for a couple of hours already, and it felt like a lot longer. The police had asked us every imaginable question about what had happened, and most of them they'd asked us two or three times. They asked us with Myra and Alan and me all together, and then they separated us and asked us the same questions again. I was really scared at first, thinking they were going to arrest us for something and send me away to reform school, but they kept assuring my dad they just wanted to make sure they got their evidence straight so they'd have a strong case against Mr. Garfield.

"What about Mr. Sloan?" my dad had asked at one point.

"I can't really talk about that," the head detective had answered.

But finally it looked like they were done with the questions, and we'd all been just sitting quietly for a few minutes. Our parents pulled their chairs up close to us and kept touching us.

I guess they just wanted to make sure we were safe or something. I almost wished the police would keep us there all night, because I knew as soon as my parents had me alone, they'd start in with the questions about the computer. I had to tell the police about that, because one thing they'd been confused about was how I was getting the messages to Alan over ByteLine. I could have made up some story about having a hand-held minicomputer with a cellular telephone hookup—there are such things—but, of course, my parents would have known I was lying.

I had watched my parents' eyes get wider and wider as I explained the truth. Finally my dad had stopped the questioning to ask a few questions of his own, about whether there was any pain involved, headaches, that kind of thing, whether I felt different when I wasn't using the head-computer, whether it affected my vision—doctor stuff. My mom just kept looking at me weird and shaking her head. Then my dad turned to the police and said, "I don't want any of this to get outside this police station. At all."

The detective shrugged. "Well, I can't guarantee that. The media—"

"I don't give a rip about the media," my dad said. "If this is true and not just some hallucination, this boy won't have a minute's peace from the tabloids. And if it *is* just a hallucination, your police department is going to look like a bunch of idiots. So let's just agree right now that this part of the story is for your records only. It has no bearing on the case against Garfield anyway."

Finally they'd agreed. But I knew my parents were going to have a million more questions as soon as we were alone.

The door opened and the head detective walked in, followed by—

"Mr. Sloan!" the three of us said at once.

He looked awful, worse even than when we'd seen him in the back of the police car. He looked tired and—well, old. He tried to smile, but it didn't really come off. Then he sat down, rubbing his stubbly chin. "I can't tell you how bad I feel about all this," he said in a hoarse voice. "Your lives were in danger, and it was my fault." He sighed deeply. "I owe all of you an apology. And an explanation," he said, looking from us to our parents. "So here goes."

He paused for a moment. "It was Mr. Garfield who set fire to the school. I was already with the police when the report of the fire came in. But what I did was just as bad. I did steal that money."

It's funny how, even when you know something is true, you can tell yourself it isn't until somebody says it out loud. Hearing the truth from Mr. Sloan's lips made me feel all hollow inside.

He took a sip from the cup of coffee he'd carried in with him. "It happened once before, when I was in college. I was going to have to drop out if I couldn't come up with some way to pay my tuition, so I just hacked into the school's system and marked my account 'paid in full.' I got caught eventually, of course. The school decided not to press charges if I paid everything back—with interest—by the end of the year. I managed to borrow enough money to do it. So I was in the clear. Except for one thing: I had learned that I could get out of a tight financial spot by using computers in illegal ways."

Mr. Sloan glanced down at the floor and sighed. "About a year ago," he continued, "I found myself in one of those tight financial spots. I was already stretched too thin, and then we discovered that our insurance was only going to cover about half of my wife's surgery. I was going to have to put the house up for sale to pay off the medical bills. I couldn't stand the thought of my wife and kids living in a cheap apartment somewhere."

He shook his head and took another sip of coffee. One of the other detectives poked his head in, looked around at all of us, and then pulled back out and closed the door.

"I noticed, just as I assume you kids did, that there was a problem with the fund-raising account. It took me about a week to figure out what was happening. Every time we entered a check from any income-producing activity, such as fund-raising, the computer would automatically revise the figures as soon as we closed the program. Then it would instruct the bank's computers to redirect some of that money into a variety of blind accounts Garfield had set up all over the place that couldn't be traced back to him. It wasn't that hard for him, considering that he had also created the programs that handled the school district's accounts at the bank. That was really the only weak link in his plan, the only way I could be sure it was him. He was the only one who knew the systems well enough to pull the scam off.

"So at that point, I had a right choice and a wrong choice. The right choice was to gather the evidence and turn it over to the police. Instead, I made the wrong choice. I altered Garfield's system at Livermore so that if somebody were tipped off, the police computer technicians could follow Garfield's tracks pretty easily. Then I went to Garfield, told him what I'd done, and asked him to let me in. I wanted some of that money—just enough to get out of debt and get back on my feet again. He really had no choice."

Mr. Sloan shook his head and gave a sad chuckle. "It's easy to rationalize what you're doing when you want to do something wrong. I figured in a year I'd be out of debt. I was going to pay it all back eventually without anyone knowing just by throwing some money of my own into the pot every time we did some fund-raising, so I told myself it wasn't like stealing, really. My plan was to make Garfield stop as soon as I had all I needed, and that would be the end of that."

"But at least," Myra said in a strange voice, "you weren't taking it for yourself. You were just trying to protect your family."

"No, Mr. Sloan's right," my dad said. "He was still breaking the law. And he was taking money from organizations who needed it—the shelter for the homeless, the children's hospital."

Mr. Sloan nodded. "Exactly." He smiled up at Myra and Alan and me, but it wasn't a happy smile. "Thanks for trying to make excuses for me, kids, but there really aren't any. It was wrong. Period."

He looked at me. "I knew that all along, but I realized it for sure when you and I talked at the convenience store that night, Jed. I went home and sat with my kids and realized how much I'd hurt all the people I loved—my wife, my own two kids, and all the kids I teach every day, like you three. So…" He took a deep breath. "I disappeared for a few days to think things over, and then I came back and turned myself in. Told the police the whole story. It was just a coincidence that while I was sitting there confessing, Garfield finally panicked and tried to burn the school down to eliminate the evidence that could have linked him to the crime. And then Jed and Myra—man, if anything had happened to you because of my stupidity…. You have no idea how sorry I am." He looked down at the floor again.

The head detective, who'd been sitting quietly over in the corner, shifted and cleared his throat. "Wrap it up, Sloan. We've got to go."

Mr. Sloan looked up. "I'll plead guilty," he said. "I'll get a reduced sentence for testifying against Mr. Garfield. If I'm lucky, I may not have to serve time behind bars at all—I may just get community service."

"All right!" Alan said.

Mr. Sloan didn't look happy about it, though. "I can never teach again," he said. "And that's the only thing I ever wanted to do. I'm a good teacher."

I opened my mouth to say, "You're the best," but nothing came out. I felt something so strongly I was shaking, but I didn't even know what it was.

Mr. Sloan looked at me a long time, then looked up at my dad. "My own fault," he said. "My own fault."

The detective opened the door, and Mr. Sloan stood. The detective took him by the elbow, and they went out. The door closed behind them. I wondered whether I would ever see Mr. Sloan again. I wondered whether I wanted to.

Chapter. 17

I took out the last of the screws and carefully lifted off the back of my computer. Yep. It was all still there. I could see the black soot on the anode at the base of the cathode-ray tube from when I got zapped.

The SIMMs—memory chips—I'd been trying to install that night still sat next to the computer, waiting. Time to finish the job.

I guess I was lucky to still have the computer at all, after everything that happened. I half-expected my parents to burn it or something. But they surprised me. My dad had taken me to the hospital the day after the fire and given me a lot of tests—an EEG, X-rays, and all that kind of stuff—but all he told people was that he was checking me for the effects of the stress and shock I'd been through. Everything came up normal.

But then, back at home, he'd taken out my first report card of the year—C's and D's. And he'd held up some of my grades from the past few weeks—all A's and B's. "I really like the new grades, Jed," he said. "We've known all along you could get grades like this. But all the same, I think we'll leave the computer turned off on school days, okay?" He gave me a look. "And if you ever want full computer privileges again—" He waved the A's. "Just keep these grades coming."

Believe it or not, that seemed okay with me. It's funny how much things can change in just a few days. I've given up using my head-computer in the classroom because I realized it was, well, cheating. And cheating hurts people. *Friends don't cheat each other,* Alan had said.

Mr. Sloan had hurt people, too.

I still think he was the greatest teacher ever. Right now, though, I don't like to think about him very much. But I've seen him since that awful night, me and my dad. We went to his house after he got out on bail. We didn't stay long, and nobody said much of anything. But he thanked us for coming, and he looked like he meant it. My dad told him to let us know when the sentencing would be, and Mr. Sloan said he would. On the way home I kept thinking, *How do you react to a friend who does something like this? I guess you try to go on being friends.*

That's exactly what Alan and Myra have been doing with me. After that night in the police station, I realized I owed them an apology too. So when I saw them next, I told them they were right—I *was* cheating when I used the head-computer at school. And then I said I was sorry. That made me feel a little better about things. And even though they both give me a hard time about it now and then, I can tell they're glad I finally owned up to what was really going on.

I could see the motherboard hiding back behind

a few cables and things. I had to unplug the end of one wide cable and then move it out of the way. It was stiff, so I carefully taped it off to one side.

I hadn't told my dad I was doing this. I figured he'd try to stop me. He'd say it was dangerous. But I've gotten fried once. I could keep it from happening again.

Slowly, I moved my fingers through the tight spaces and reached for the motherboard.

Putting the SIMMs in wouldn't really be that hard, once I got the motherboard out where I could get at it. All I had to do was take the old SIMMs out and put the new, higher-rated ones in. Easy. I touched the edges of the board with just my fingertips, keeping as far away from the anode as I could. Then I wiggled the board just a bit. It seemed to be stuck. I needed a better grip. I thought, *Maybe if I work my fingers just a little further in, being careful to avoid that anode, of course...*

"Jed!"

I jumped about a mile. My heart was pounding. "What, Mom?" I said, trying to sound normal. She was standing right outside my closed bedroom door.

"Alan's here," she said.

"Okay. Tell him I'll be down in a minute."

I'd forgotten. We were going to get together at Todd's with a bunch of other kids to watch the Cornhuskers game that afternoon. "Just you wait, little SIMMs," I whispered. "I'll get you guys in there yet. After all, you cost me a lot of money." I reconnected the cable and screwed the back of the computer in place.

I grabbed my Cornhuskers cap and ran downstairs. There by the front door stood Alan. And Myra. Myra looked up as soon as she heard me, and her eyes got bright, but her smile was shy.

"Have fun!" my mom called.

"I didn't know you were into football," I mumbled to Myra as I pulled my coat on.

"Forget football," she said. "I thought of something more important."

"There isn't anything more important," Alan said. "This is the Oklahoma game!"

Myra waved him away impatiently with a

mittened hand as we headed off down the sidewalk, our breath smoky. "Imagine yourself ten years from now, Jed," she said. "Suppose you were a trial lawyer, like my dad. You'd be unbeatable! You'd have your entire legal library right at your fingertips during the trial. *Nothing* could come up that you couldn't handle. Or in business—in negotiations with another business person, you'd have resources he couldn't begin to match, no matter how much research he did. Or you could go into politics. Just think of the advantage you'd have in a debate in Congress!"

My gosh. She thought like a grown-up. Scary.

"Yeah, great, Myra," Alan said, "but what do we do in the meantime? Who wants to wait ten years?"

"Let her talk, Alan," I said.

Myra stuck her tongue out at him and smiled back at me.

Alan just rolled his eyes. "Weird," he said.

Yeah, it *was* weird. But like I said, it's funny how much things can change in just a few days.

Nobody ever looked at me that way before.